REDDITCH AS IT

Redditch as it was

by

Lily Norris

Illustrated by Christine Cater

BREWIN BOOKS

First published by Brewin Books, Studley
in October 1990

©   Lily Norris 1990

ISBN 0 947731 77 6

This book is fiction and no reference
to real persons living or dead is intended.

Typeset in 11pt Baskerville
and made and printed in Great Britain
by Supaprint (Redditch)Ltd., Redditch, Worcs.

To Les
from

Lily Norris.

Chmnter Cate.

DEDICATION

A tribute to my parents
Minnie and Ernest Cater
and my own family
David, Terry and Cynthia

ACKNOWLEDGEMENTS

Thanks to Edna Thornton, Mary Gibbs, Joyce Waters,
and Marjorie Mathew, also the many kind folk for
their thoughts remembered.

CONTENTS

The old Lock-up which was on the corner of Red Lion
Street (Now the site of the New Civic Offices)

CHAPTER ONE

LOVE IS NOT TIME'S FOOL

Val tucked her deep auburn hair behind her ear for the hundredth time this morning. The strangled note of a distant cuckoo called its muted cry and Val thought the faint calling sounded incongruous so late in the year.

She always welcomed the incessant song in early spring when the snows had melted and a misty veil shadowed the blue bell woods bordering Scarfield Farm, but now in July it seemed out of place.

There being only the frozen emptiness of winter before them, nevertheless, she was thankful Alf didn't have to go to war, and, although the usual disillusionment of Mondays were felt, it soon wore off as she planned her day.

The immediate task was to organise the pile of washing into separate bundles. The "whites" to be washed and boiled in the copper, then the "woollies" and last of all Alf's overalls. She never wasted any precious soap-suds for, after all the laundry had passed through them they were then used to scald the drains and back yard. Alf had already brought in the vegetables and she could hear the sound of his heavy boots over the unmade road as he bustled back to the yard. An urgent cry from the baby had deprived her of giving Alf a "cheerio" kiss.

The twinge of disappointment was eased by Topsy's angelic smile as the golden-haired baby lay snuggled in the crook of her arm.

The baby soon slept peacefully by the careful rocking and although it had taken but a few moments to replace the sleeping form back into her cot, when eventually Val went downstairs, Alf had gone. Before bed last night he had told her that it was necessary to be at the farm early. He had to take the wagon into Birmingham to fetch a piece of machinery. From the outside brewhouse Val could see the steam escaping as the laundry was scalding in the copper. Mary her eldest daughter could be heard shouting at the boys to get ready for school. Val had to pay Webbs today and

1

decided to fetch the shilling piece Alf had promised to leave under the pillow, but after again climbing the stairs and turning over the pillow, found only a half-pence piece.

She muttered impatiently as she wildly sought to find an excuse to tell the baker. She prayed he wouldn't stop delivery.

"The bab's awake again Mam," Mary called.

"Yes, I know. I'll come up and turn her on her side until you're all gone to school," Val shouted up the stairs and with some concern called to Edward, "Put your thick blue jersey on Edward, it's quite chilly out."

Mary was left to deal with the porridge and Val put a loving arm across the thin shoulders saying,

"You're a good girl, our Mary," then hurried out to give the boiling washing a business-like prodding thinking 'another sprinkling of Hudson's powder then they can come out,' she then cast an expert eye on the small clouds gathering over Bill's mother's house.

A brilliant blaze lit up the kitchen-cum-dining room showing the well scrubbed deal table; the cheerful pegged rug designed as a huge red rose, the industry of their courting days. The polished cheeks of the grate sparkled with a brash show of Val's elbow grease!

Alf must have collected the last of the snap-dragons while he was up the garden and Val noticed that he had stuck them unceremoniously in an old jam jar, but this did not spoil the handsome red, gold and russet colours. Val soon arranged them artistically in the brown crock jug and placed them centrally in the jutting bay-window that gave a clear view of the lane leading away from the hamlet up to the school.

The smell of hot buttered toast still clung to the room when, about an hour later, Val waved to the three figures from behind the flowers. She watched earnestly until the threesome merged with Clarry Bailey's children from the further cottage along the lane. Edward and Tom walked with their heads close together studying some gem in the smaller boy's hand, but Mary stood back as if disgusted at the object of their discussion.

Val waited until the group melted into the distance then cleared the table and went immediately to bring down Topsy. This wasn't her christened name but Alf had said when he first saw her,

"She looks a real Topsy," so the name remained. She had been christened Minnie Eliza after Val's mother.

Passing the first landing window Val noticed small blobs of wet on the pane and mumbled

"Oh, goodness! Alf's shoes are still outside." She ran downstairs and hurriedly snatched them in from the downpour. As though she was looking at them for the very first time she noticed the odd shoe-laces, the split at the seam and, across the instep the mis-shaped leather bulge where his swollen second toe bone had thrown the shoe out of shape. She pressed her lips to the well-worn uppers, then scolded herself severely for being so sentimental.

The diversion was only momentary and while near at hand she crossed to the brewhouse to agitate the boiling laundry for the last time and went upstairs again to attend to Topsy. An acrid smell of soiled diapers rose from the cot but, once bathed, and re-gowned the cheeky grin, so like Alf's, crumpled the innocent features and soon the baby was kicking merrily in her pram. As she put her down Val whispered tenderly,

"Topsy is my darling." Not daring to indulge too long in the magic baby games Topsy was given a bottle of milk and placed quite near to the window where she could watch her mother working.

By mid-day the washing, having been well rinsed and starched, was now blowing in the fresh, warm breeze after the morning shower. The thin small items were placed here and there over the golden hedgerow to get the benefit of the open air and sunshine. Val had picked up the Indicator and read - "When the boys come home have ready a pair of Huin's slippers." She would try and get a pair for Fred her brother. She thought 'War, war, war. Why did men have to fight?' The next news was a bit more cheerful. 'Lord John Sanger's Circus coming.' That would interest the boys, especially Tom who loved animals. Reading on she mused ambitiously on to the farther announcement, 'Four Freehold houses for sale near town centre producing £65 yearly. Selling price £715.' She put the paper away as Topsy gave a cry, who, seeing the table laid for dinner shouted,

"Piece, piece." Val sliced off an "outsider" from a Webb's cottage loaf, smothered it with butter and handed it to the child to keep her quiet until dinnertime. Mary won the race to be first home and flung her arms around her mother's neck, while the boys struggled to get through the doorway together in an effort to present their mother with the results of their morning's work.

Unabated the chattering went on as they found their places at table. They always waited for Dad to say Grace. Washing day's ritual menu of cold cuts and milk pudding to follow did not appeal to Tom and he fidgeted as he enquired

"Where's Dad? He promised to show me the new

rabbits. I wonder if he's gone straight up the garden. Can I go and see Mam?"

"No, he'll be here directly. He's always ready for his dinner. He loves his beef and pickles." Tom, not usually surly, grumbled,

"I'm never allowed to do anything."

"Sanger's Circus is coming to town. That will be a treat for you. That is if you behave. I'll put it to your father directly he comes home. Now just sit still for a while longer," Val said.

She sliced off a few pieces from the new cottage loaf and whispered.

"I wish he'd hurry up. Get dishing up, Mary. I'll give Topsy another crust of butter to stay her a bit longer." Mary's hands shook and the floury, boiled potatoes split open as she energetically pounded them into a creamy mash with butter and milk.

"Don't worry, mam. He won't be long." And even as she heard these comforting words Val knew Mary too, sensed some alarm.

It was nearly half-past one when the two figures stood at the door. Val trembled as she saw one was Mr. Edwards, Alf's boss from Scarfield Farm and the other, Sergeant Banner from the local police station.

There had been an accident at Beoley Brook. The cart had turned over and Alf had been crushed. Mr. Edwards' voice softened as he tried to console her by saying,

"He died immediately."

CHAPTER TWO

VAL'S SURPRISE

The austere manor farm provided a solid background to the landscape viewing it from the rear of Val's cottage, and could be clearly seen when winter turned the fruit trees into bleak spikes but, at this time of the year the abundance of fruit and foliage of the apple and pear trees hid most of the farm buildings which stood a good half-mile from the bottom of the orchard.

Val looked at her wrinkled hands as she waited for Bob Sellars to call. He had told her he would be collecting the sewing machine today and at the thought of losing one of her most valued possessions her heart was really aching. Her mother had made a supreme sacrifice to give Val the handy piece of equipment to provide an easy cheaper way of keeping the young ones decently clothed.

They were growing so fast and Mary had the figure of a young woman. Val smiled at the thought of the slim delicate form, so loving, so innocent.

It was coming up to the second Christmas without Alf. There had scarcely been any time for grief because of her double work-load, caring for the children, animals and garden. Perhaps the over-loaded schedule was a disguised mercy for the fullness of each industrious day combined with the extra devotion from the children and her few relations and friends enabled the grief-stricken young wife to enjoy deep health-giving sleep most nights. She agreed heartily with the written text that "Of all our desires - love it was the best of them, but sleep worth all the rest of them."

Only the primitive urge for the children's and her own survival eased the raw wound of her husband's untimely death. After months of sadness a gentle, merciful stillness pervaded her mind and now a clearer dawn soothed her broken heart. Although the crevices in her cheeks portrayed the stress of her loss, her tall slender figure, proud bearing and natural dignity had not been destroyed. Not even the aeep grief could erase that silky, creamy like skin or alter the gentle sweetness and tenderness of her true self.

Selling the machine seemed to be the last resort in order to provide the extras for the coming Yuletide. Bob was usually ready with a joke, but Val was not up to his brash repartee this cheerless morning. She opened the cupboard under the shallow, stone sink and began to tidy the pots and pans stored there in an effort to shake off the void and desolate mood of loneliness. This comfortless self-pity was only a momentary spasm and a childish squeal from the back garden brought her quickly to her feet and rushing to the door she saw Topsy chasing the butterflies from the tall, spiky Michaelmas daisies. The air was filled with the maturity of autumn and the thistle heads spread their fluffy strands everywhere. The bees droned heavily among the heavy ruby heads of the peonies while the golden patch of corn in the distance, and the thoroughly sun-drenched flower border, gave that voluptuous fragrance of fulfilment.

The dreary ordeal ahead was forgotten in the scene of wanton delight as the peacock-blue of the border flowers vibrated with the scarlet of the child's dress. Val had left the chores and skipped over the uneven paving slabs making her way to where the sound of tinkling laughter could be located. She had crossed the yard noiselessly, and kept well within the shadow of the cottage where the overgrown honeysuckle gave off its musky fragrance, so as not to disturb the child. From the apple tree she plucked one of the sweet doddings to please the little girl.

It was here in the garden that Bob found her when he called to collect the sewing machine.

"Oh, there you are Val. I've been knocking the back door. What are you so engrossed in?" He glanced over her shoulder to see the antics of Topsy. "She's a bright one Val. Looks like a sugar dumpling. Look at those dimples and gold curls. She's going to make some young man's heart glad later on, I know." Then taking a more serious tone and holding out his hand to steer her over the broken stones he asked, "How are you coping old girl?"

"That depends on each day. Everyone has been so kind, but while this evil war is still on everyone is in the same boat. We're all getting tired of bone soup. As you know I've had to sell a lot of my precious belongings but, the machine is not a luxury Bob, it's a necessary part of my home. It has allowed me to earn a few pounds extra. It's going to be a wrench and a great strain to part with it. Also I could do without the useless advice and sarcasm from her up the road."

"I know what you mean. Sometimes I wonder if these people have any imagination at all. She must know the extreme difficulty you have making ends meet. Even the new farm hand has been on the receiving end of her sharp tongue. She can be a bitch. Like Bill Ganner said this morning, 'Her wants gooin' oove.' "

Val sensed a malice never shown before by the neighbour, no doubt taking the machine away gave him no pleasure at all. It was obvious there had been some soul searching for he choked with unmanly emotion.

"I'm sorry, Val." In the end it was Val who had to perform the consoling gesture to make the whole miserable affair bearable; she touched his arm and said,

"It's not your fault lad."

After a while Bob explained that there would be a machine going for sale in next Friday's auction.

"But I'm used to this one Bob. Mother's generosity proved a recompense. It seemed to bring me luck. I could weep at losing it, but tears are such useless things. Mother entreated me not to cry. She said 'The Lord may send you something worse to cry for.' I've remembered her words, I'll count my blessings instead. But don't let me see you take it."

"Orders is orders, Val, you stay with Topsy and I'll load it onto the trap if you have agreed with Mr. White to auction it. But come up to the sale at Church Green on Friday night. Promise me." He pinched her cheek and muttered, "Buck up, old girl. Worse things happen at sea."

"I know, but I feel so vulnerable. You take it Bob. I'm going up Unicorn Hill to fetch some faggotts for dinner."

He passed her later on in the lane and shouted over the clatter of horses hooves,

"Don't forget Friday." Val felt a measure of warmth at the concern in his voice but in a matter of fact tone answered,

"I'll think about it." She knew full well that she would be at the Mart on Friday night, if only out of curiosity.

That next Friday dawned dry and bright, so Val took full advantage of the weather to make the house spotless for the weekend. By midday all the beds had been changed, the bedroom linoleum washed with disinfectant and carbolic soap, for the influenza plague was still rife. Only last week Philip Spencer from the council house had died. With a sigh of relief she gave the last stair a good polish and gazed with satisfaction at her handiwork. 'That's half way house' she thought. The small sitting room did not demand so much energy: the rug to be shaken, and a quick sweep around the floor and ornaments dusted. Windows were thrown open to let in the autumn sunshine and fresh air for an hour or so. The heavy labour was the family room. She had raked out the cinders and the soot earlier, sifting the ashes to separate the clinkers to be used later. All the individual rings had been removed and the collected soot from underneath brushed into the ash pan at the bottom of the fireplace.

After all the top plates had been washed with hot soda water to get rid of the grease the range had been subjected to a good layer of Reckitt's black lead and now shone fiercely complementing the massive freshly scrubbed deal table top.

Val now had to clean the windows with vinegar and warm water, take down the velvet curtains for a good shake in the garden and then onto the heavy chore of scouring the brick floor yard and drains. The time was getting on by the time the curtains had been re-hung, the flowers re-watered and the ornaments washed and replaced on the high mantle shelf. It was nearly midday, she was on the last patch near the solid back door scrubbing merrily away when Mr. Edwards called to leave a box of 'golden drop' plums. That meant jam making this afternoon but that wouldn't take long once the children had gone back to school and Topsy was having her afternoon nap.

Val was indulging in a quiet doze after the morning's weekly clean and saw the future a little rosier now for, with the extra money from the sale of the machine she would be able to make plans for Christmas and, at this moment Mary came in carrying Topsy.

After tea Mary said she would put the boys to bed and Val had already fed and nursed Topsy until the child's head fell forward in sleep. A while later Val slipped on her out-door coat and hurried the length of Windsor Road. At the bottom of Prospect Hill she noticed a familiar figure with the usual scarf covering her curlers.

"Hello, Nellie. Are you going up to Church Green? I was nipping up to see what my machine fetched. The machine had to go to the auction to get some extras for the holiday."

"What a shame, kid, you needs that machine." Nellie Ralp's friendly brown eyes betrayed real sympathy and went on, "No, I'se gooin' to me mam's. Er lives in th' house th' other side th' eagle. They's killed a pig at Bentley and me auntie arst me to give 'er this fry for some faggotts." Val slowed down to keep pace with the older woman whose heavy figure steadied as the hill gradually got steeper, and as they neared the Crown Inn Val asked,

"How's Ron? I heard he was brought back to Hewell

last week. How's his leg?"

"Yes. He's gone to Hewell. Mrs. Huins is doing a wonderful job settling them in and giving comfort to their families. He's 'ad one operation over there but he's against losing it altogether. I think it will come to it eventually, but, he's terrified of not being able to dance again. Ye knows what a one he was for 'is dancin'. I was just doin' me manglin' when me mam cums dane to tell me. He cum back Monday but I en't 'ad charnce to see im yet. Me mam said he'd been left three days in the open before they found 'im and gangrene set in. P'raps they can save it now he's yum."

"I do hope so, he's only a boy, his life before him. I see in the Indicator, Tom Smith from Withybed has been wounded. It would kill Jim if anything happened to that lad."

"There's plenty o' rumours gooin' round, but I'se 'eard it'll all be over by Christmas."

"I do hope so. I'll slip round to see him Nellie when he's fit enough."

"Thanks Val, how's your little uns?"

An unkempt boy rushed from Ma Riley's shop half way up the hill. Nellie stepped back and shouted to him,

"Keep out o' the 'orse road, Billie." Billie Court leapt on to the safety of the pavement and sped off in the direction of Albert Street like a deer.

Nellie tugged at her head scarf, her voice full of concern,

"You must find it 'ard gooin' Val. Why don't you get wed? You really needs help with them mites to feed and clothe."

It was painful to even begin to explain the loss of Alf's caring protection. Not for one moment could she envisage any other soul replacing Alf. The complete unity they had shared was unique. During the last lonely months she had re-lived their happy times together, even at her busiest, an odd memory would merge with the daily routine to bring a tear or a smile. In truth, their short loving marriage was another world away, but the black despair of each morning without him at her side gradually faded into the past as the shared thoughts of companionship and tender moments of courtship had all been exhausted.

The evenings spent at Bosworth's cinema on Church Green and long walks through the Abbey meadows and leafy Worcestershire lanes; all the penny pinching and saving in order to get married in style. All the precious thoughts were savoured until with an inborn common sense Val saw her life as a woven tapestry and realized this was part of life's rich pattern. She gripped the cross at her throat thankful for the radiance of the perfect love she had known. Only she, and she alone knew the deep anguish and misery of that dreadful accident, and, although the void had grown less frightening the wound was still sore. The children's needs had pushed her along each day as each season brought different problems. At last she glanced sideways at the kind dough-like features of her companion and quietly said with simple endurance,

"No one will ever wed me Nellie, I'm still wed." Nellie nodded thoughtfully saying,

"Yes, I know." Changing the line of sadness she told Val "Mr. Cornforth, the Redditch Post Master will collect walking sticks for the wounded soldiers. It says in the Indicator he wants to collect at least two thousand. I think me mam's still got that one me dad used when he was alive. I'll get it off her tonight."

At the top of the hill near the Crown Inn they parted.

"Cheerio Nellie. Sorry I've been so wrapped up in my own affairs but I'll see you at Hewell Grange on Sunday."

"Cherio Val. Keep smiling."

Nellie carried on up towards Izod's Yard while Val crossed over Easemore Road just as the clock struck seven. A strong smell of mildew struck Val's senses as she stepped into the unheated room of the small annexe behind the main auction room, her light steps echoing as she tripped across the bare floor. Thick cobwebs hung like curtains across the iron-barred window and the dark brown paint was peeling from the paint work which seemed as bleak and poverty stricken as the poor people gathered there. A pathetic sight as soldiers' widows and orphans stood stoically waiting in the ill lit building watching their few possession disappear for practically nothing, for by the time the auctioneers had deducted their bonus there wasn't much left for the seller. Val thought: 'Cashing in on people's despair. Too miserly to even keep the place clean.'

The main hall was full of potential buyers, mostly farm labourers and their wives anxious to pick up a baragain. Val suddenly felt awkward. Nevertheless, Bob's jovial laugh could be heard and she was glad when he came towards her, hands outstretched in welcome.

"Your machine was first on the list, Val. It went for one and a kick, so I bought it back for you. When Mary starts work you can think of repayment. Until then it's well worth what I gave for it to see you cheerful again." he chided.

Val felt absurd and tongue-tied with gratitude. She found it difficult to hide her pleasure, but she remonstrated,

"You could have bought it for your mother." She smiled in an effort not to seem ungrateful, but embarrassed by such kind unselfishness.

"Mother has one, Val. I was determined you should have it back when I saw how distressed you were last Monday."

"Thank you, Bob. But," she tried to sound stern, "don't impoverish yourself for my needs. I must stand on my own two feet. My mother forever reminded me 'as you make your bed - so you lie on it.' I only came out of curiosity just to see how much it would fetch. I think you've pulled some strings somewhere." Val's voice held a quiet joy.

He winked and with a rustic abruptness and hint of apology said,

"Come on. The trap's in the yard. I'll give you a lift home."

The tortuous uneven pathway through the gulley that led through Hemmings' Entry made Bob stumble as, although not a cripple, a kick from a fractious horse had broken his ankle and the bone had never set properly. He made no spectacle of the injury but Val felt a sudden qualm of pity as he quickly tried to set his balance.

Falling leaves covered them like confetti as they cantered home in the trap along Scarfield Lane. They were both laughing loudly when Mary opened the front door. She had laid the table for supper and Bob stayed long enough for a bite and a drink of home-made wine.

Bob coughed into his fist several times as Val enthused about Bob's good deed for the day. He tucked into the slab of cheese and hunk of bread Mary had sliced off the new loaf, he polished off the wine in one swig. Mary refilled his glass, as he showed some embarrassment at the uproarous delight of mother and daughter.

Mary whispered in his ear,

"I think you are going to be a favourite person for a long time."

"I'd hate to see her out of work," he said good humouredly. With one accord they laughed loudly. Then Bob winked at Val saying, "I'll see you tomorrow evening Val."

Although Val was thrilled by the comforting bond between them that had grown stronger today, she wasn't sorry when Bob decided to go. She shook him by the hand warmly, her face beaming with happiness and said,

"Goodnight Bob, and thanks again."

Clinging tightly to the machine later, she couldn't wait

to revel in the delight of hearing it whirring merrily away
once more.   It was stupid she told herself to attach so much
importance to an inanimate possession but, she gripped it
affectionately smiling at Mary, and the girl too, found it apt
to indulge in a pat and a term of endearment for the small
useful object.

"Things are looking up now, Mary.   I've already chosen
a colour for your new dress.   This is my life Mary.   Thanks
to Bob, now I've got it back I can make the new curtains for
the big house and have some spends for winter holiday."
Mary agreed and gave her mother a smothering embrace
saying,

"You look ten years younger, our mam."

CHAPTER THREE

VAL'S NEW JOB

It was Tuesday of the following week and Val stood on the steps of Clarry Bailey's house half-way down Brockhill Lane.

Through the sky flecked with a grey ripple of cloud the autumn sun rolled over the town in the distance. In the heaven a gentle breeze urged the clouds slowly on towards the west but over the farm cottages here, the breeze blew quite strong bending the crowns of the willows and poplars, ruffling the stream and chasing droves of crimson leaves along the lane.

When Clarry answered the door with flour-covered hands Val felt a sense of guilt at the thought of asking the favour of her friend which she had in mind.

There always was much disorder in the home of Clarry, but she was such a warm comfortable soul, that, at one raising of her eyebrows or impish grin and all her faults were immediately forgiven. A true Irish charmer with such a command of the Gaelic tongue that her turn of phrase naturally became a comedy. She had often said to Val that life is a tragedy to those who feel and a comedy to those who think.

"I'm a great thinker, Val." she had often exclaimed even in the midst of the many dreary days of wartime.

Val followed her into the living-room and thought she had better get it off her chest straightaway and told Clarry,

"I've come to ask you a favour, Clarry. I've been thinking of getting a job while the children are at school. Do you think you could look after Topsy for me? She's a good child and I'll only be away a few hours." Val searched her friend's face for the least sign of dissent but there was none and Clarry answered without hesitation,

"Sure. I'll be glad to. She'll play with Bridie. When do you start?"

"Well I've already had my hands tested for needle

sorting and I'm going up now to get the results. If all goes well and you are agreeable I could start this coming Monday." There was a note of optimism in Val's querying voice.

Clarry had already poured the boiling water onto the tea leaves, and Val, out of habit, had set out the cups. As Clarry squeezed by to get to the small kitchen she gave Val a gentle pat saying,

"Don't disturb your head further. No bother. Just bring the mite over when you're ready. Bridie has taken a light sickness of the chest but didn't Mrs. Clements give me a bottle of her cure-all? The congestion is not cleared yet, but they can play indoors. You leave Topsy here now. Your legs will travel faster without a burden."

The two children threw a furry ball backwards and forwards on the rug before the coal fire and as Clarry warmed a flannel dipped in goose grease she explained,

"This is an ancient remedy, Val. The smell would sure make a spy talk, but it works wonders, that's the main thought."

Val remembered her own mother's favourite cure for chesty coughs and gave it out now to Clarry,

"Cut up a Spanish onion Clarry, and layer it in a basin with demerara sugar if you can get it. The syrup is liquid gold. It's strong stuff but it's powerful."

"I have heard of doing onions that way. I'll try it if the cough persists. They seem to be playing contented enough now. They can stay there awhile. You slip up town. See if you can get me a bit of fish from Harry Turner on the market please Val. I'll pay him on Friday, tell him."

"Righto dear, I will. You are an angel. I'll get us some bread too if they are queueing, although I don't like the colour of the bread from Sanders. It must be the soya or potatoes they mix with the flour. Have you heard Clarry that the war could be over by Christmas?"

"Not too soon for me. Now away with you. The sooner you go the sooner you'll be back.

"I won't be long. Thanks again Mrs. B."

"Oh, away with you."

Once past the sweet scented lavender hedge she made her way towards the station watching out for queues which she could join on the return journey. Her pace quickened as the unmade road joined the newly surfaced Hewell Road, here the road levelled out before she came to the Enfield Works and she was able to move quicker. Sadie Thornicroft passed on the other side of the road sporting a gay, straw hat.

"Been to Birmigham, Sadie?" Val called out. Sadie cocked her head and looked away.

14

"Now what have I done to her?" thought Val.

They told her at Milwards that the test had proved perfect and that she could begin the following Monday morning. Again a sense of hope and relief as Val foresaw some enrichment for her family's welfare.

Val collected the fish from Harry Turner, but wasn't so lucky with the bread, although Sanders had a notice to say that bread would be on sale after two o'clock. Passing Morriss's shop Val noticed a sign saying 'Trap for Sale. Strong springs. Four pounds' and wondered if ever the day would come when she would be the proud owner of a horse and trap. The very idea seemed so distant the thought was cast from her mind, and she hurried back quickly to tell Clarry the good news from the Milward's office. When Val got back both girls had been fed and were peacefully sleeping in the boy's bedroom on the ground floor overlooking the front garden.

"You still cooking, Clarry? Lovely smell." Val ventured.

"Just a few jam scones for the boys' tea. Those kids are always hungry, especially our Michael. I don't know where he puts it."

"He's growing fast. Can I use your la pomme, Clarry?"

When Val came back into the room she told Clarry,

"You've got no lock on your lavatory kid."

"Mother o' God. There's nothing worth stealing in there," came back the reply.

"You're always on the go Clarry. Why don't you relax awhile?" Val asked her friend.

"Yes. But I never get anywhere. I don't mind cooking, but I can't abide housework. I do it for the simple reason that you couldn't get in the place if I didn't. If it moves - I feed it, if it don't - I dust it and if it cries I kiss it. That's my philosophy Val and I stick to it. I'm not organised like you. Wait 'till I tell you. This morning I went upstairs to fetch Bridie's pinafore down, found the pearl button off big Jim's shirt, decided to sew it back on, then changed Michael's bed, opened the windows and clean forgot what I went up for. Anyway, girl, how did you fare up town?"

"I've got the job and I start Monday." Val threw her arms around her friend's chubby figure, "Thanks to you Clarrybell. Can I leave Topsy asleep until Mary comes home? There was nothing at Sanders, but they will have bread this afternoon. Has Webbs been yet?"

"Yes, Tony was happy. He had heard also by the end of the year some of our troubles will be over. Sadly his eldest brother was amongst the wounded they brought to the station on Monday. He said Thomas had got off light considering some of the poor lads he'd seen there." Clarry's usual smile vanished as she remembered he had also said there could be mass unemployment.

"Hope and pray Val. As long as I have two eyes to see and two hands to work that's enough for me."

"Those poor men," Val said inwardly criticising herself for chasing after riches while thousands of young soldiers, many limbless and sightless were having to come to terms with their grim, bleak future. There was a deep thread of irony in the saying, 'Win 'em and wear 'em (medals) - like the soldier with the wooden leg.

"I promised Nellie Ralph I'd go over to Hewell Grange on Sunday. Will you come with me Clarry? We can take some of that golden drop jam we made."

"Yes, yes" agreed her friend, "Jim can borrow the pony and trap from Dixon's. Mr. Giles won't mind when we explain our errand. Val made for the back door saying on the way out,

"Cheerio, then Clarry. See you Sunday. I'm going to push the house over now and get it all ship-shape before I start at Milward's factory.

Later Val was indulging in a quiet moment's dreaming, trying to decide whether to buy a new saucepan or that material she had seen advertised in Hollington's at 1/11 for a yard, when Mary came bouncing in with the baby chasing behind. Webbs had left her two large cottage loaves and a small brown loaf in the brewhouse. So with the pork dripping Clarry had shared with her, the remains of the fruit cake and the yellow jam they all enjoyed a lively tea.

The boys had brought home a new friend called Harry. Behind his ready grin there seemed to be a smothered sadness and when Val asked concernedly if his mother minded if he stayed to tea, with bent head and crumpled features muttered fiercely,

"I ain't got no mother. She went away. There's only me and my dad." He met Val's sympathetic gaze and went on,

"My dad started driving for the Lavender Laundry last week. We've got the cottage next to the Baileys. It's lovely here after living in Birmingham. We only had the horse road for a playground." So Val told him cheerfully,

"You are welcome here anytime. Tell your father we are only country folk, but he need have no fears for you while you are with us."

"Thanks Mrs. Thomas. I'll tell him when I get home." With that he dashed off to find Edward and Tom who had gone to feed the animals.

Bob showed his friendship in many ways those first sad years without Alf and Val came to rely on his constant support. When she told him that evening of her intention to start at Milward's there was a vague note of apprehension in his voice as he queried,

"There's not much intelligent conversation in the factory workshop Val. Are you sure that you can cope? The atmosphere isn't too healthy and some of the labour force a coarse lot. I've had to take parcels before now to Milward's and the language of some of the women, it would make your hair stand on end. But you know best Val. Perhaps it won't be for long."

"Better than an empty pantry and smoke-less chimney Bob. It will only be part-time to begin with. I know they have an absorbing interest in the commonplace, but prouder women than me have made the work place respectable. While they are talking about me they are leaving somebody else alone." Before he left about nine o'clock she had convinced him it was for the best.

Bob had told her the end of the war was only a few weeks away and a new surge of optimism invaded Val's heart. Earlier in the spring Bob had spent all his spare time setting out the vegetables and plants and thanks to his country upbringing there would be a good harvest.

Val marvelled at his patience with the boys. When she called them in for bed they told her of his ways of teaching a laying hen to rear some goslings from the fertile eggs. They were full of the tales he'd told them.

"He put the eggs in a bucket mom and the dud ones all fell to the bottom. It's magic," said Edward, quite impressed by the movements in the eggs which held the live chicks.

"I'm going to be a farmer. It's wonderful to see the re-creation of the animals and birds" said Tom in wonder.

Although there was still some daylight, due to the new clock timing, Val insisted they should go to sleep at once lest they should keep Topsy awake.

CHAPTER FOUR

VAL STARTS WORK

This was the day before Val was due to start work and she had an urgent load of work to be tackled. Mary had taken the boys to Sunday school and Topsy was asleep. She had been very tiresome; when Val tried to clean her face she had resisted every movement. Then she seized the bowl and tipped it over Val's clean overall. For that deliberate offence Val had slapped her, her rarest remedy, and already Val felt some guilt. The copper had already been filled for baths and their clean school clothes airing on the fire guard when they came back.

"I've just seen a two-er" declared Edward. Val looked at Mary puzzled.

"We saw a lady with twins at a christening" said Mary. "Our Edward couldn't take his eyes off them."

"Who was that Mary?" Val was curious as she turned over Edward's thick school jersey on the fireguard.

"I'm not sure mam. Their mam didn't look very old. The vicar named them John and Sarah, but their surname was the same as their mother's single name Mrs. Field told me. Now I'll get the boys' tea as they can go to bed early tonight. You will have to see if Granny Ross has a coat to fit our Tom, mam. He looked a sight today. Everybody was staring. This coat's too short, and not very warm. Feel it."

"Yes, I know. As soon as I'm paid Friday, I'll go to see what she's got in. I'm worried about the bab. There's a slight wheeze on her chest today. Hope she's not sickening for the measles."

"She'll be alright mam. There's still some Ipeccacuanha Wine left from Ma Clements. I'll put some warm water to it, that will clear it overnight."

The following morning was clear and dry. 'Good drying day' Val thought as she dressed Topsy in the woollen leggings. "Keep still darling" she begged as the chubby legs escaped again and again from Val's hold.

"Don't want to go to Clarry's" Topsy whined peevishly.

"Yes, you do. You and Bridie can have a picnic under the plum tree. You'll love that. Now give me a kiss and promise you will be a good girl for Auntie Clarrie." Topsy grudgingly obeyed and was soon at the back door trying to reach the "catch".

Once Topsy was safely in Clarry's care, Val headed for Milward's, and as she negotiated Fish Hill prayed earnestly for the safety of her loved ones while she was absent. At the factory, Edna Brough showed Val the factory routine and she soon settled down to the job given her. It was deadly monotonous but it gave Val time to mentally balance her budget and, as her deft fingers swiftly sorted out the faulty pieces of metal for scrap, so she reckoned up her family needs for the coming week. Three bags of coal that would be one and sixpence. Two quarts of lamp oil and some candles - fourpence. The flour and yeast about two shillings. Soda for scouring and washing fivepence and a farthing. The usual tea and cocoa - sixpence. Some fish and bits of bacon - one and sixpence. Then some margarine at fourpence. There would be enough butter made from the free milk from the farm for their bread.

Perhaps she could manage a small joint of beef this weekend and Clarry could come over to share it. Val was deep in thought and carefully manipulating the extra cash from the factory and, had come to the point where she felt satisfied to know, at last, she might make ends meet.

Phil Clements sidled over to Val's bench and putting her arm around her shoulders said,

"Don't look nay kid, but you sees her over on the far bench, Winnie, her's knocking it off oov George Wilkes out of the scouring shop. He's married, got three kids." Val did as she was bid and kept looking down at her work. Now Phil Clements never stopped talking. It gushed out like hot air from a gas pipe. Senseless garbage most of the time. The woman was completely and absolutely unaware of the damage she might cause to the people involved. Val gazed into the woman's inquisitive eyes and wondered at the poverty of her mind. Not many workers believed her tales but they say there's one, at least, in all the factories. Sometimes she was boring, sometimes malicious and very, very seldom there was a grain of truth in her stories. How she found out the minutest detail of nearly everybody's business in the local vicinity, no one ever knew. It seemed she surmised a great deal, and the most distant details not readily available were merely invented.

A dangerous tongue, but Val found light relief in the

silly gossip and Phil's local slang gave her sayings some unique humour.

"I've been trying to see how best to spend my wages this week. My eldest lad needs a new coat, Phil. But this week's wages on Friday will provide the extra," Val confided.

"I'se gotta tell yu this kid. You woon't get any wages this week. They keeps a week in 'and. You'll ave to work two weeks before you picks up any money. I can lend you a few shillings to go on with," she said helpfully, but Val declined.

"No thanks. It's good of you, but no." Val thought, within ten minutes the news would have spread all over the market town, but it was a blow. Poor Tom, he'd just have to wait for his coat.

The sudden change in Val's situation, coupled with the fact that she had thrown her whole energy into the morning's labours proved too much for her and the strain proved obvious, for the foreman passing along the bench shouted,

"Are you alright, Val?"

"It's the strain of a new place. The smell of the oil and grease and the noise of the scouring machines made me feel a bit faint."

"You look a bit peaky. It'll wear off." He sounded sincere, but Val knew he was a busy man and with all the women working there, had got used to women's funny turns.

"You'll be alright after a cuppa," he consoled over his shoulder as he hurried away. Val was asked to contribute a penny for the tea.

"It'll do next week if you haven't got it," Dot Hemming told her. The collection provided tea and a drop of milk, but sugar was in short supply so someone had suggested treacle as a sweetener. This did produce sweetness, but turned the liquid a deep purple colour. Val thought it resembled the farm duck pond, but it was hot and refreshing and Val drank greedily. Nevertheless, she was very pleased when the lunch time bell sounded and she was able to breathe deeply of the fresh air. She almost ran home anxious to see how Topsy had behaved for Clarry. There was no need to have worried for Clarry had sorted out all Bridie's playthings and Topsy was delighted to be the centre of attraction while she felt poorly.

Back at the work shop the afternoon's atmosphere had improved. The windows at the end of the shop had been opened to let in the weak autumn sunshine. The job she was put on was an easier routine and, as she whispered to Edna as she passed her chair on the way to the toilet,

"It's good to be at work to have a rest."

"Make the most of it. You may be on swivels

tomorrow," Edna said. The factory environment produced a natural condition of bleak monotony and life was only made bearable by adopting rowdiness or worse still this holier than thou state of normal respectability from which evolved a narrow, enclosed, almost vicious society that would not tolerate any deviation from what they regarded as normal behaviour. The hard core of the work force only wanted to be regarded as eminently respectable neighbours. Consequently it was a local religion to peruse the local newspaper to see who had been hauled up Church Road to the police court room. There was an older lady started Milward's the same time as Val. She was a true comic and kept the girls in "stitches". Regular outbursts of raucous laughter brought the foreman out of his office several times the first day, but as long as the workers got the orders out he never exercised his authority.

Lizzie Gibbs (the new lady) sat next to Val on a high stool.

"I keeps slipping off this bloody thing," Val heard her moan under her breath. Then turning to Val said,

"I put some of them new silky drawers on this morning and I keeps slipping abate on this high stool."

"Put a flat cushion on it" Val advised. But that didn't work and again she would shoot sideways. Lizzie had to take a packet of needles to be marked off and from the office Val heard her shout,

"Ooh! Bill, if you touch me there you'll have to marry me." The whole shop roared. The women that worked there tried to make a miserable existence bearable and apart from the background of eternal silly gossip some of the more imaginative women ran shoe-draws, sweeps, lotteries and one clever girl did a crochet service which included even coats and shawls. This was very popular with any young lady collecting for a 'bottom drawer'.

Nevertheless, there was a mad dash for coats at the end of the day. Winnie came out with Val and asked,

"How's your first day been, Val? I'm going as far as Hemmings Entry. I'll walk with you."

"This morning seemed unsettling but this afternoon did not drag too much. But it looks as though Lizzie won't keep her place too long if she keeps up those capers."

"She'll simmer down. The money is needed. Her eldest son, Richard has been gassed. The effects are terrible. It's affected his lungs. He's lucky he's back home, but Alfred her youngest is still at the front. Her old man spends all his money at the Greyhound. She never knows where the next meal is coming from."

21

"Edna Brough came over to help me but to be quite frank I was so glad when she decided to help elsewhere. She's so insecure. Whatever is the matter with her? I said to her, 'Do you knit Edna?' "

"No, I'm no good at it," she said.

"Do you like cooking Edna?"

"No, I'm no good at it." Most innocently I enquired,

"Have you any children Edna?" Bill was going into the office at that moment and he shouted,

"No, she's no good at it. Are you Edna?" I begged her to ignore him as there were other compensations and told her to look on the bright side! I gave her my mother's repeated promise that, 'if one door shuts, another door opens:' I tried to cheer her, but it was hard going."

"Yes. We all know her and have tried to bounce her out of this sad depression. Her husband was reported missing a few months ago and she's been like this ever since. She'll budge out of it as time goes by." Before they parted at the bottom of Hewell Road Val had explained the loss of Alf in the accident and of the constant struggle to get even the bare necessities.

"Well, Val, I run a shoe-draw and when your turn comes up you can spend the full amount at Humphries. Considering the never ending replacement of children's shoes I should have two or three draws then you'll always have some credit. It's only a shilling a week".

Val willingly accepted this offer which proved helpful. They parted promising to meet next morning and walk to work together. Winnie had said that she could get some vouchers straight away as Bill Walker wouldn't mind waiting another week for his turn. 'At last' Val thought 'a light at the end of the tunnel'. Mary had collected the baby from Clarry's and Val could see straight away she had brightened. Clarry had brushed the child's hair into a winged coil of an old fashioned style, but Val soon altered it into the wavy fringe. She didn't want her darling turned into an adolescent too soon. The two boys and Harry were spread eagled across the living room floor listening to the crackling radio Bob had set up for them.

"When that story has finished go into the garden. You are allowed an hour or so before bed," their mother sternly ordered.

Val gathered up the baby and stumbled over the boys boots scattered across the back door step as she went outside to sit and nurse her to sleep while the sun lasted. As they swayed they looked like two drunken lovers and Val glared at the three inert figures but decided not to chastise the culprits at that moment. Later the children came out to play hop-scotch while Val nursed Topsy under the lilac tree. Val watched Tom's dexterity as the agile footsteps gave him superiority in the first game. She thought then he would make a fine dancer for the order of his footwork was decisive, light and accurate as he cornered the squares marked across the yard. Val felt lazy without some chore to occupy her fingers so she put Topsy to bed and picked up Tom's overcoat to repair it once again. The familiar sound of Bob's horse trotting along the drive made the children forget their games.

"It's Bob, it's Bob, I want a ride" Edward shouted.

"And me, I want to feed the horse. I've dug up some carrots especially," Tom sounded more mature.

"All of you stay where you are until the horse stops," warned their mother. "You might frighten him, all shouting at once." Bob saw to it that they had their ride then went on up to the vegetable garden.

"I'll get you some spuds up while its dry," he told Val. "It won't take me long. See you in a minute." He laughed loud and long later when he had asked Val how her day had passed at Milward's, and she retold the story of Lizzie shooting off her stool every so often.

"They all seem helpful," said Val, "but I feel a stranger. I suppose that's only natural. There was spite in one old lady's remark as she noticed my patched skirt. But that's the least of my worries. Winnie advised me to let it go in one ear and out t'other. We'll see what tomorrow brings." Bob showed her a peg doll he'd made for Topsy. "That's sweetly pretty. She'll love it. Just the thing to pacify her when I leave her at Clarry's in the morning. Thanks Bob." Changing the subject he said,

"We're playing on the Crown Meadow on Saturday Val in aid of soldiers and sailors fund. They are getting the parcels delivered well now. I had a letter from Bob Smith. He wrote to say how welcome the parcels were and to give sincere thanks to the people responsible. Anyway the match should be lively. It's the singles gainst the marrieds."

"I expect the singles will win, they don't have any worries" laughed Val.

"Don't you believe it."

"Now Bob, be serious. What worries have you got?" He held his gammy leg in the air.

"What about this? I could have been out fighting." She looked at him pensively quite sorry for his explained predicament. He had never mentioned it before, but Val noticed by the pained expression how deeply it affected his outlook.

"I'll find you a nice young lady, Bob. There's some fine girls at Milward's. You know how they describe the girls of our town. 'Poor, pretty, but proud.' I'll get you fixed up for a date." Bob went silent.

Mary had rounded up the boys for bed quite a time ago, Topsy was fast asleep and Val could see Mary's head bent over her tapestry work studying the last awkward emblem. From the 'long field' came the sound of sheep and along the rough cart track leading to the farm a lame soldier and his girl strolled arm in arm lost to the world. Here the walled-in area was still warm from the evening sun but Val had finished sewing and said,

"I think we've had the best of today Bob," making a movement to go indoors. Bob gathered up the chairs and scarves left by the children and as he gathered up the para-phernalia said to Val,

"If you cut up some rags we can finish that rug indoors."

"That's an idea. It will make a smart addition to the sitting room for Christmas. I've got another podger. We can start on the blue border, we can cut up Tom's overcoat after I've been to Granny Ross's." Her pride forbade her from informing him of the disappointment she had felt when she knew about the system of holding a week's wages in hand.

It was while the house was quiet, except for the con-stant pulling and poking of the tools as they both tackled the unfinished area of the hessian cloth, that Bob murmured,

"I don't want a silly young girl Val. I want to marry you." It was obviously an effort for him to make such a grand announcement. The voice seemed alien with its ultra polite tone.

"I know it's quite soon after your loss, but with the war still on I can't bear to see you shouldering the difficulties of these hard times. We are foolish to waste more time. You must know how I feel Val. Say 'yes' and we'll be wed early next year. It's a decent enough time to wait."

Val, not showing surprise although she was taken aback by his sudden seriousness, answered.

"No, Bob. I'm too old for you. There must be ten years difference."

"That's no matter at all." Val felt his arm around her shoulders as he kissed the thick hair coiled in the nape of her neck. She rose effortlessly not wanting to embarrass the man further.

"I'll make some cocoa" said Val. She didn't have to

witness the struggle he endured while changing chairs for, when she came back into the living room, he was already laying out the plates for supper.

During the long, bleak months after her loss, Val had been subconsciously aware of his devotion but the stubborn fact of the age gap would not be erased.

"We'll see" was all the words she could honestly utter when she met his querying gaze. His support would be greatly missed, and the fellow's cheery company was taken for granted by the children. By his own admirable character a special niche had been formed in Val's home, and yet she could not bring herself to give a definite commitment. That night he didn't stay too late and after Val had let him out and locked up, she cleared the supper things away and going into the scullery noticed Bob had already washed the vegetables and placed them neatly in their separate saucepans. The care and tenderness this displayed made her glad that she had promised to meet his mother at the Homestead on Sunday.

During the first week at the factory Val came to know most of the girls. The two Browning girls were not very forthcoming but Winnie had told her that their mother was very strict.

"That doesn't stop them from conversing" said Val, not quite understanding their retarded behaviour.

"Are there any boy friends hanging around? The thick root of Ada's nose is poorly made. It doesn't make for beauty. But her deep blue eyes would fetch a duck off a pond, and Emily too can be quite sweet when she smiles."

"Well, Val. Ada did have a nice boy but her mother put her foot down. They are pampered to death. No one's good enough for her daughters. But I think it's just a mania. She doesn't want them to leave home. So they come straight to work and straight home."

"That's a bit dull for two young girls," said Val.

"Yes I know. And I've seen it happen afore they're the sort that gets into trouble."

"Oh, well" Val mused, "it takes all sorts to make a world." Phil Clements had kept her up to date whether Val needed to know or not. You had to have it, about the goings on in the factory and out of it. With her usual unwelcome familiarity she would sidle up to Val and relate the whisperings of the grape vine saying,

"Kid. Has you 'eard the latest?" Val would usually listen half heartedly saying at the latest outrage,

"You should take care what you're saying Phil." But the gossiping creature would complete her barrage. Of course Val provided a fresh and green audience so the woman was in her element. This morning's tea break was alive with the rumour that Bill's wife had found him giving a message to his lady love by pouring so many buckets of water down the yard. Apparently there was hell to pay and Winnie heard his wife shout,

"I'll have your bleedin' guts for garters." And what she intended to do to poor Gladys was nobody's business. That's why her's not 'ere this morning," Phil told them. At last, the foreman came to break it up and Val from proven experience tried to ease the atmosphere by saying,

"If only these girls would realize it's never wise to change horses in the middle of a stream. They are simply exchanging one set of problems for another, if they did but know it. They wrongly think they are getting a better deal, but if they leave a chap who drinks, perhaps the other one gambles or has some other weakness. No one's perfect. If they are looking for someone perfect, they must go to the grave-yard and dig one up. But they never listen." Phil wasn't listening either, and even as she worked, pressing and moulding the metal, her inquisitive eyes were darting here and there enveloping the whole work shop with a swift all seeing sweep.

CHAPTER FIVE

CLARRY'S SWEET DISORDER

Clarry's house was the image of a carefree happy home. It was poor, but never cheerless, perhaps it was Clarry's volumptuous figure that blinded one to all the disorder of the warm, sincere smile that illuminated her face in welcome. Her smile seldom vanished, it was perpetual, like a settled dimple; the twinkle was an inheritance from her forebears from the emerald isle. Everyone knew that the tin marked flour on the high mantel shelf would hold sugar. In the one marked tea would be a collection of buttons, and the one marked savings - nothing. It might hold a few shillings each Saturday when James was paid, but it never stayed there long enough to be called 'savings'.

The long centre table of the living room served many uses. Through the morning's turmoil of food being eaten, meals being prepared for later, and the take away packets being prepared, the immediate activities left not a spare inch of space. When the miscellaneous collection of plates, dishes and wrapping paper had been stored away, so, on came the baby's bath water; then later, cooking utensils; nothing very complicated, just a pastry board and Clarry's method of making pastry was with a bottle. She said it made the pastry lighter. She had no scales, for there was no need for them. Clarry just threw in the bowl as many ingredients that were available and hoped for the best. Then getting near to dinner time all the same plates, dishes would appear again, and the routine would begin all over again.

But this was early afternoon when Mary called and poked her head round the living room door.

"Who owns the big eye?" shouted Michael. He hadn't gone to school because his other pair of boots was at the menders.

"Don't be nosey," said his mother. "Mary's waiting for our Angela." Mary saw that today the room was a picture of extraordinary homeliness and, added to the usual array of tins and bottles was a glass jar visibly displaying a set of grinning dentures and alongside an obviously out of work toothpick. The roaring fire blazed from the black-leaded grate, its cheeks shining boldly, while the black family pot gurgled quietly at the fire's edge sending out a delicious aroma of beef broth. The deal table was laden with an assortment of thick cups and saucers ready for tea.

Mrs. Bailey was busy at the sink, "Nearly tea-time, not a tattie peeled, not a sausage pricked," she confided to Mary, then louder she shouted at Michael,

"Go and see what Patrick is doing, and tell him to stop it," but Michael ignored her as he concentrated on the job in hand. He was squat on the pegged rug before the fire-place, his short, ginger hair burnished by the flames, his chubby face contracted with dedicated perseverance. He groaned as he battled on, his pointed ears, agonised expression, and his smothered squeals and frenzied move-ments gave him a fiendish appearance. Mary looked down to see what was so urgent, and watched him determinedly pulling out the faded stitches that held the uppers to the sole of his left boot. A sigh of relief sounded as at last he managed to wriggle his toes through the mouth he had made.

"Look mam, my boot's worn out," he cried in a devilish attempt to rile his over worked mother. But the poor woman endeavouring to peel the potatoes, stir the broth, and nurse the baby tried not to hear him. He squawked as she nearly trod on his fingers.

"If ye don't move from under my feet, I'll take a rod to ye me lad. Move." He gathered up his feet sadly defeated by her indifference.

"I have a need for some food, mother."

"Ye'll have to wait for tea. It will be ready soon."

"I'm hungry now."

"Be quiet," Clarry ordered, "or I'll rattle a stone off your heels."

"I'm starving hungry," he persisted.

"You can't be," the woman said.

"I am," he argued.

"Well, what do ye want?"

"I'll take a slice of that," he said pointing to the slab of fruit cake recently taken from the oven. His mother looked aghast as she said in surprise,

"It's fruit cake. Ye know full well ye don't like fruit cake our Michael."

"I do."

"Ye don't."

"I do."

"Ye don't," Michael's mother insisted.

"Well, I do now," he pleaded, a bored look on his face.

"I'm not giving ye fruit cake. Ye only waste it." The boy attempting to destroy the rest of his boot lashed out at the sleeping cat, there were two loud squawks, for the cat scratched back in immediate defence.

"I'm hungry," Michael wailed.

"Well, hurry up. What do you want?"

"I've said a dozen times, I'll take a piece of that," again pointing empahtically to the cake sitting on the table.

Mrs. Bailey sent up a fervent prayer for strength.

"Well, ye'd better eat it all or Mother of God, I'll truly beat the living daylights out of ye." She took a bread saw, hacked off a piece of cake, and put it on the stool near to his hand. Michael did not notice it at first, being too interested in collecting hairs from the cat's tail.

"I'm starving hungry," he again agonized. Mary told her mother later that he sounded like a parrot but more distressed.

"There it is by you, on the stool. Eat if ye're starving hungry."

The cat decided to laze elsewhere and Michael was carelessly pushing the cat's hairs through the fire bars when the sharp pains of hunger must have struck again. Then he saw the plate of cake. He picked it up and scrutinised the offering, and as if recognizing some nauseating object, his face changed colour and wrinkled with pure disgust as he hissed,

"What's this our mam?"

"It's fruit cake. You said you wanted a piece of fruit cake."

"Fruit cake! fruit cake! You know I don't like fruit cake our mam."

Then Angela appeared and Mary said she was glad to leave before the blood ran. Mary was already a clever mimic and she imitated Michael's indifferent question,

"Who owns the big eye?" with studied emphasis on the eye part of the question.

Val laughed uncontrollably at Mary's account of Michael's behaviour. Mary told her mother that Angela had fixed the day for her wedding and had asked Mary to be bridesmaid.

"It will be a month today at Mount Carmel, so that will give you time to make up that material you bought last week. Will there be enough to make it ankle length?"

"Yes, plenty. I'll gather it at the hem and pockets to give it a bridesmaid effect. Will John be invalided out by then? He only came back last Monday."

"I suppose so, Angela has made all the arrangements. We're going over to see him at Hewell tomorrow. They're having the reception at the village hall. I hope it goes off alright. You know what the Baileys are when they get together."

"They like their wee drapee" Val mimicked.

"The quality of their sober language is charming, but, as you say, when they're in their 'cups' the language becomes more fruity and the civil niceties are forgotten. It won't be a big wedding because of food shortages and travel problems. Angela is such a sweet, quiet-voiced girl. Let's hope for this one day there will be agreement in the camp."

"I'm sure there will be. Clarry will keep them under control, that's if she too, doesn't indulge. She's not used to wine, not too much anyway. Don't bother your head Mary, just enjoy yourself. Your main concern will be Angela's appearance and comfort. The weather should hold out until then. I've too much work to do here, but I've promised Clarry I'll care for Bridie while the wedding is on. You must tell me all about it when you come home, and we'll have the photos. I'll probably let Bridie see Angela and John wed but we will not be able to stay long. I'm positive Angela will look devine. That beautiful auburn hair, and with her vitality and wit I'm sure it will be a day of wonderful memories.

"Surely hope so," said Mary as though uttering a prayer.

The few weeks passed too quickly for Clarry for she told Val she often wished there were more hours in a day. Angela's wedding day dawned bright and clear, not too warm and although Bob Sealey had forecast a frost, the prophesy did not materialize.

When Mary returned in the evening it was a lively tale she had to relate to her mother and the boys. Every detail was related blow by blow. Mary began,

"Angela with the help of Mrs. Bailey, me and sister Annie appeared superbly serene in the cream satin dress made by her auntie across the water. Friends and relations sacrificed some of the meagre rations from their own homes to make the wedding feast as spectacular as any war time wedding could be expected to be. With the knowledge of previous Irish weddings, the priest had let out a few subtle hints before the service, but it was at the village hall reception afterwards that the sparks began to fly." Mary said that the tables were all loaded with homely victuals laid on by well wishers.

Firstly Mary explained how the chairs scraped over the shiny wooden floor of the hall as the guests arranged themselves coyly at their allotted places, and the bride and groom and close family made for the top table.

Mr. Bailey stood up clutching a glass of his best elderberry wine kept for the occasion and called for quiet from the noisy assembly. They all rose murmuring religiously,

"To Angela and John."

Mary told how when the guest on her right was served with the plate of ham, so thinly sliced that you could see the pattern on the plate, said,

"I could put this in my hollow tooth." He was apparently somebody's Uncle Horace, for the words sounded occasionally,

"Pass the salt, Uncle Horace,"

"Move up a bit, Uncle Horace." His appearance, according to Mary was very unusual for in an attempt to hide the hairless area across the middle of his pate, he had scraped the thin hairs from the wide parting over the skin showing on the top which only emphasised his baldness.

"Poor man," said Mary. "He walked as if every bone in his body ached. His wife, Rosie, no great beauty grumbled,

"This pig ain't so young as it used to be."

"Once the bride picked up her knife and fork it seemed to be a signal for action," Mary said. She was aghast at the dexterity of the hands flying in every direction and from different areas of old Ireland came the various accents in some delightful lilting sing-song voices,

"Pass the porter darlin,"

"Where's the Worcester Sauce?" Then Mrs. Muckle a neighbour, her face quite rosy snorted,

"There's no boiled eggs left in the salad."

The best man complainingly stared at the chitterling plate before saying,

"All gone, gannets!" Michael shouted,

"What's a cure for sea sickness Uncle Horace?" Uncle Horace couldn't reply immediately as his overworked gums were doing overtime, on a pork hock. So back came the answer from the tormentor,

"Bolt down your food of course. Oh, never mind." And then it was Horace's wife, Rosie who piped up,

"Just look at that fizog, will yer? Looks like an unmade pudding. Enough to make the toothpaste go back into the tube."

Mary wasn't sure to which of her neighbours she referred, but there was quite a few that could have fitted that description. Rosie was a well known tough character. She

31

had small, steely eyes and a sharp bitter tongue. Mary told her mother that the bitchy sneer had turned her mouth into the resemblance of a mouse trap. No lady whatsoever."

Val knew Rosie Fowler. Life's frustrations and unrewarding grind had caused a misplacement of her features. So she was not surprised to hear of her comments. Mary said,

"You could hear her nagging voice above all the rest," and mimicked,

"I knows her. Knowed her family. Bad lot." "I never heard her say a good word to, or about, anyone all afternoon. She makes herself look so ugly. Her mouth too made up, like a slash of beetroot. I bet when she goes to the zoo they give her two tickets. One to get in and one to get out." Mary said,

"Don't be too unkind Mary," although the jest did have a ring of truth in it and, at Mary's apt description, Val couldn't help but smile.

Then Mary said,

"There was this old maid aunt there Miss Slater. Our mam, you should have seen her. Quite often I heard her request, 'Pash the Guinness, pleash.' One uncaring youth passing behind her chair nearly dislodged her dentures. 'I wish you would exercise more caution, my good fellow,' she wailed. But it was when the Miss Slater's dress was described that Val really laughed out loud.

"Her feathered hat was askew and her eucra-lace dress so tight across the bust that it seemed any minute those lace covered buttons would bounce off and shoot everybody within range of the third table. She was quite merry by four o'clock and wanted to find a victim to join her in an Irish jig, but the more sober guests managed to dissuade her." Val had heard these celebrations ended up in a fight due largely to the fiery temperament of the Gaelic nationality.

"After most of the home brew was supped," Mary said Mrs. Bailey noticed the tension and was seen gripping the tablecloth with both hands.

"I distinctly heard her whisper," 'Somebody get the bride's mother out.' Auntie Nell sitting next to her nervously plucking her ruff collar simpered,

"But you are the bride's mother."

"I know," she answered sharply, "Get me out." Her pleading was uncharacteristic but she really meant it, Mary recalled.

"It was a lovely wedding. It's a shame they are so quick tempered, especially today. I think Eddie was a bit over fortified. I heard him say to the Auntie Annie,

"Why don't you go home?"

"Never in a month o' Sundays. Never, I'm not going home," she argued. "I gave that bride an expensive present. I'm enjoying myself. It's a treat to enjoy something you've paid for, even if it is once in a lifetime." Mary finished the story in fits of laughter as she fantasised somewhat towards the end, putting on an adult imitation to keep the boys laughing. With a twinkle in her eye and many funny grimaces she went on lying through her teeth.

"The priest's face changed colour from a benign grey to a reddish purple. It appeared he was in the grip of some powerful emotion. Michael, having tired of trying to dislocate the back leg of Miss Slater's pet poodle lay flat on his back under the table and had placed some lighted matches quite close to the priest's cassock. Father O'Malley set up an unnerving scream which vibrated through the hall and quickly disappeared into the back room telling the world he would demand a replacement of his vestments."

At the very end, Mr. Bailey stood up manfully, reached out to steady himself on the centre pillar but missed and fell flat on his face. Mrs. Bailey lifted her pinched tormented face to the ceiling and prayed.

"Mother of God Be with us all. May our husbands never be widowers." The guests realizing the wedding was over, discreetly stepped over the contented Mr. Bailey and disappeared sideways into the dark. Many of us younger ones stayed to clear up the mess but honestly our mam I've never seen a wedding like it. Luckily Angela and John were miles away before the 'troubles' had started.

CHAPTER SIX

VAL'S NEW FRIEND

"The Lavender laundry van's here" Val shouted to the boys, who were sorting out their football gear in the outhouse. The driver of the laundry van was Harry's father. Val had never met him, but from the long accounts by Harry who idolised his dad, she had formed a picture in her mind. Mr. Hendley collected the laundry from the main farm house every Monday and then gave the children a lift to school. This morning Edward would not get a move on and soon Val saw Harry's father coming up the path. He had a dull job but, here was no dullard. She knew he was not old, but the slight stoop gave him a middle aged bearing. Ten years ago, Val thought, before care and grief had caught him unawares, he would have presented a truly handsome figure. The impeccable manner, studied movements and energetic vitality made Val wonder why he had made no grand advancement in life. His features held a sweetness that seemed almost unnatural for such a strong utterly masculine person.

It was not for Val that special gentleness, for he was looking hard into the lilac tree at the back door. A lively scuffle came from the depths of the greenery as two starlings fought for supremacy. When she had opened the heavy, back door, he offered an outstretched hand in friendliness, and Val, warmed to the firm, steady grip, as he enquired if the boys were ready.

"He's never been so happy. Sorry I haven't been over before to thank you, Mrs. Thomas," he apologised.

"Harry's always welcome here. I see now from where he gets those solemn chocolate drop eyes," and realizing the hidden sadness extended the welcome to himself.

"You too, if you care to come over, Mr. Hendley. Bob Sellars will be glad to show you around the farm and small holding. Of course, since my husband died we have had to reduce the livestock. But the poultry and rabbits have made good replenishments for the larder while this war rages."

"Yes, Harry told me of your husband's accident, but I see the tragedy hasn't completely injured your independent spirit." He looked over the well kept buildings and the distant orchard and remarked knowledgeably,

"You seem to be managing very well."

"Bob Sellars does give us a helping hand whenever he has free time."

With that Edward, Tom and Harry came rushing into the yard anxious to get into the van for the exciting ride to school.

"Bye bye, Mrs. Thomas, glad to have met you."

"Bye bye, Mr. Hendley. Please come to see us again."

But he never took up the offer and Val often pondered over the implications of his wife's disappearance. As his laundry collections included the factory Val occasionally caught sight of the heavily built, sad figure moving around in the yard. Beneath the man's natural charm she sensed a bravely borne misery and longed to show her willingness to help but, on the few occasions they met at work, Val was so shyly aware of her soiled, shabby overalls that it was impossible to search beyond his friendly enigmatic smile. Last Friday she had rounded the reception desk hurriedly, as usual, and actually bumped into him. He touched her forearm lightly but immediately shrank away and the conversation was senseless,

"Oh, Mrs. Thomas. How nice. How's the family?"

"Very well, thank you."

"Time flies, must dash, see you," and he was gone. After many efforts, Val became more and more perplexed and understood the loss of his wife must have caused a deep suffering, but failed to see reason in his casual behaviour. He always sent thankful messages via Harry, for the boy was so regular a visitor to Keepers Cottage, that he was almost part of the family. But Mr. Hendley had such a curious effect on Val that even the mere thought of him brought a swift dampness to her eyes, therefore she always gave a loving welcome to his son, in an effort to show she cared. As the autumn drew on Val was too occupied with her own growing family to give much time to Mr. Hendley and his private grief. Her sisters were quite generous and, if it was made known that she had any needs, the help was usually made available, although Val's fierce streak of independence forbade much acceptance. Janet her younger sister was vivacious and caring, but Ethel, her eldest sister, absurdly blamed Val for her misfortunes. Ethel was overpoweringly 'generous', especially with useless advice. Strangely enough the advice so freely handed out never included any expense or inconvenience to herself, and Val reconciled herself to the fact no real help would come from that quarter. She actually overheard Ethel say to Janet one day,

"It's all our Val's fault. She's not a good manager. She could make the children's shoes last a lot longer if she wasn't so fussy." Val often dwelt on that silly remark. How could anyone cramp and ruin the growth of tiny feet for the sake of saving money she asked herself.

It was then that she realized Ethel did not completely understand the issue, for having no offspring herself saw no cruelty whatsoever in damaging someone else's children. Ethel's house was immaculate, because Bill, her husband was at the front, which enabled her to work long hours at Terry's factory on ammunitions which paid well in the early war years. This gave her a fine spending power with which to equip her home. She even possessed the new fangled gadget, a washing machine, Ethel called it. She said it replaced the old dolly tub method, but Val wasn't too impressed.

Val never felt welcome there lest the boisterous children should cause some damage to the showplace, although Ethel was always shown great love and welcome when she did condescend to visit Val's cottage, and Val put up a special effort to please her sister.

There were usually small gifts of home-made rhubarb jam or bottled fruit available for her to take home. Ethel intended to pay a visit this Sunday and Mary had already washed and starched the bright yellow curtains so that the humble abode gave off a shining welcome, well able to withstand a visitor's critical scrutiny.

Val rose early on the Sunday morning and noticed the roses heavy from overnight rains were pressing their heavy heads against the kitchen window, and looking through their foliage Val relished the sight of the heavy fruit on the elder tree, remembering the useless piece of folk-lore that lightning never strikes a house where elderberry grows which gave her some measure of comfort. Out in the garden geraniums and dahlias were all dripping wet, but the Michaelmas daisies still stood defiant and starry eyed. It was well after lunch when Ethel knocked on the door and no sooner was she indoors she carped,

"Our Val, why don't you shorten Tom's trousers? I've just met him up town and he looks a disgrace in those ill fitting garments."

"They are a bit long Ethel, but he feels the cold and these autumn winds are searching. This weather reminds me of the October fair. Will you be going to the Stratford mop?" Val asked trying hard not to take offence at the sarcasm in her sister's nagging.

"Why don't you buy him some that fit properly?" Ethel went on. How could Val explain that they were hand me downs from Harry Hendley, but she deliberately ignored the senseless, selfish remarks and lovingly said,

"Come on, Ethel. Take your coat off and make yourself at home." Ethel painstakingly disrobed of a fashionable, cossack style coat and said,

"Thanks Val. Hang it up carefully. Mind the boys don't finger it. It was quite expensive."

"I'll put it on my bed Ethel. They won't go in my room. Ethel you've got your dress on inside out."

"Yes, I'm afraid it might get marked with jammy hands." Ethel explained.

"Well!" said Val wonderingly, "I'll go to the bottom of our stairs."

In the cosy sitting room Ethel's eyes scanned every inch of the sunny coloured curtains and while expertly handling the material enquired,

"Where did you buy this from, Sages? It's a good linen."

"No," said Val hiding her annoyance at her sister's mercenary valuation.

"Mrs. Edwards has renewed her lounge furnishings. You know what a size her lounge is. She gave me the old ones. Mary and me brightened them up with an old gold dye and shortened them. There was enough material for all the cottage. Aren't I lucky?" But there was no congratulations forthcoming from Ethel, she merely sniffed at the thought of such charity handed out to her family, and if she felt any glow at Val's good luck she didn't show it, but went into every detail of the new ones she had ordered and had especially fitted throughout the house in Glover Street. She gave all the boring figures of costs, measurements and colours right down to the last farthing, so that Val was glad to announce tea was ready.

"I want the house to look cosy when Bill comes home. He wrote and said all the lads were looking forward to coming home Christmas when their leave was due." Ethel went on talking right up to the minute when Mary poured her tea into the thick utility cup. Val saw her look of disdain and asked Mary to give her the china cup from the cabinet, and cutting some dainty bread and butter said,

"Christmas is a long way off Ethel. A lot can happen at the front before Christmas. I'll be glad to see our Fred back home safe and sound, I can tell you."

"He might be back before then if the talk of the armistice is true.   Lloyd George gave a broad hint that the signing is a matter of weeks.   They were saying at Miss Rice's shop yesterday that we shouldn't have to queue much longer.   But you never seem to have to queue, yet your cupboard is always full," Ethel remarked jealously.

"We are quite a family Ethel.   Patricia shows her sympathy by saving a few luxuries for the children."

"That's a fine excuse.   I can't starve just because I haven't a family."   Val weighed up the figure of the well nourished, plump girl's appearance and against her good nature ventured,

"You don't go short of much, Ethel.   Let's pray it will soon be all over.   Did you see this pretty dress our Janet made for Topsy?   Look how cleverly she's embroidered the bodice."   Ethel gave a cursory glance and indifferently grumbled,

"She's got more time than me.   Anyway, I never was much good with a needle.   If I've got any spare time I collect some out work from Clarke's factory."

"Oh, Ethel, you are a scrat."

"Well, someone's got to keep the home fires burning. You've got Tom and Edward to help you."

"There's not a lot they can do.   They feed the chickens occasionally, but you can't expect them to sacrifice their games for dreary jobs.   They need their playtime, Ethel."

"Mary is my right hand, although there are no hard and fast rules laid down in this house.   She genuinely enjoys cooking and housework.   Of course, she idolizes Topsy, always knitting and caring for her.   Such a blessing to me. She's an angel.   She's too willing.   I have to discreetly plan outings for her.   They all went to Treadgold's yesterday.   It was a Charlie Chaplin film showing.   The break did her good. She said they laughed their heads off at the funny little man with the bowler hat and walking stick."

Ethel helped to side the table after tea and Tom and Edward joined in to assemble the jig saw Auntie Ethel had brought them.

It was a pleasant family evening and about eight o'clock Ethel asked for her coat telling Val that she had to be up early the following morning.

"I've got a parcel of pins to take back to Morrells."

"I'll come with you as far as Easemore Road then you have only to pass through Alcester Street and you will be home."

"Thanks, Val.   I'd be glad if you would.   I don't care much for passing Biddles house, all those dogs kick up such a racket."

"I'll get you jam from the pantry. You'll enjoy that rhubarb and ginger Ethel. Just like mother used to make."

Ethel waited in the fire-lit sitting room. Topsy was sitting on Mary's lap listening to a story. Topsy was learning the first letters and Mary spelled out patiently, 'A for apple. B for Bear, grr grr, C for cat, mieouw, mieouw.'

When Val came back Auntie Ethel was gazing thoughtfully at the domestic scene and Val felt a twinge of pity, for there would be no chuckling laughter or singing in the cheerless place in Glover Street. Later walking together up Prospect Hill, there was no envy, but Val did feel conscious of her shabby old fashioned coat in contrast to her sister's new outfit, for all that the younger girl's step was lighter and more energetic.

The people were strolling along the Parade and Val saw Mrs. Merry.

'Don't stop Val. I like to keep to my own set," Ethel begged. There were times when Val's pride revolted against Ethel's assumption of superiority to all other people.

"But I must," said Val. "Didn't you know she'd lost her son last year on the ship Cameronia?"

"The Lord giveth and the Lord taketh away," Val heard Ethel mutter without feeling, as they came nearer to Mrs. Merry.

"Hello, Hattie. How are you? This is my eldest sister Ethel. Her husband Bill is still away although you get regular correspondence. Isn't that true Ethel?" said Val trying to draw her into the conversation.

"Yes, yes," Ethel murmured anxious to be going. Hattie said,

"We have started a fund at the factory. Mr. Edwards from the Cricketer's Arms gave a pound. It will all help. We did have a letter of thanks from Alf Duffin. He said they received thirty three parcels of clothes and boots. He said it's dreadful being penned up as prisoners, and that they have to do all kinds of work for three pence a day. Poor chaps." Lowering her voice she whispered,

"Don't look now Val but there goes Fanny off down Birmingham Road, complete with white handbag. What a disgrace." They all three looked at the church until the powdered and painted Fanny passed by, Ethel held her nose high and caught her sister's arm urging Val,

"Come on Val, it's getting late."

"We'll have to love and leave you Hattie. Keep smiling," Val told Mrs. Merry, her voice full of real concern.

"Cheerio, Val. See you around, Cheerio Ethel. I likes your coat." But Ethel was half way across the churchyard.

When Val caught her up she demanded of Val,

"Why do you stop talking to that scruffy Mrs. Merry? She looks as though a good wash wouldn't do her any harm." Val's patience was wearing thin.

"Look, Ethel. I can give you an answer but I can't give you a brain to understand. Her appearance is a cry for help. She's a remarkable woman to have got over her loss. It must have broken her heart." Ethel's mind was dwelling on affairs more rewarding for, almost immediately she told Val,

"They are offering good money at Allcocks for fly-dressers. I'll go and see Bill Fraser tomorrow to see if there's a place still vacant. I'm fed up with the women at Terrys."

"I'll bet they're fed up with you," thought Val realizing only too well the shallowness of her sister's frivoulous nature, but not wishing to annoy her further said,

"You'll be alright now Ethel. I'll leave you here. I'll take a short cut behind the Post Office in Church Road, it won't take me long to slip over the common. Don't take on too many commitments. Money's not everything."

"I know but you might as well be miserable in comfort." That last phrase summed up Ethel's outlook on life perfectly.

The sisters embraced and as the dusk was getting more pronounced Val put a spurt on and skipped quickly over the common, not easing up until she came to the end of the lane and she could see the lights on in Clarry's cottage feeling safer as she neared home. When Val got indoors the children were all in bed, except for Mary, who was darning Edward's socks for school the following day. The fire guard was hung with the children's underclothes to be well aired before morning.

Bob had called while she had been out, Mary told her that he had brought in vegetables and some fruit for Monday's dinner.

"That was thoughtful of him," Val said thankfully. The wheels of her daily routine were oiled so unobtrusively that the pattern formed in a very agreeable constructive progress as his tenderness and care showed in so many small ways.

The days of that autumn had sped so pleasantly that the young widow envisaged a contented future with Bob. She vowed the children's welfare would be her first consideration but already they welcomed him as a mate and confidante. She closed the outside door firmly as if saying goodbye to a shadowy period.

CHAPTER SEVEN

THE GRAPE VINE

Passing through the scouring shop Val heard Phil Clement's familiar chant,

"Does you know, kid?" Val couldn't see who was on the receiving end, but the tirade went on,

"They says Charlie Field has had his house gas-tarred inside and out to get rid of the bugs." Her loud cackle sounded as she followed on,

"Now they says they's all gone next door. Well kid, I 'ad to laugh."

"At it again, Phil," Val chided as she passed by. The women were working like blacks even this early.

"Ah, Val I wants to see you."

"Later, Phil, I'm late already. I'll see you dinner time." Val was in no mood for her aimless gossip so early in the day, for she was out of coal and remembered there would have to be a trip to the gas works for coke before she went home that day.

Thomas her younger brother had seen her empty coal house, for she had swept it out including the last grain of slack. He jokingly mentioned,

"You'll be had up for hoarding, Val. I'll bring you down a couple of barrow loads before the weekend." The boys had gathered some branches from the spinney but they wouldn't last long. Her mind was fully occupied and it was quite a while before she noticed the new girl sitting near Lizzie. She heard the foreman call her Joanne.

Val envied the calm self assurance as she sat there swinging her silk clad legs, giving George Hartles a dazzling smile she queried,

"Will I be a success?"

"You would be a success anywhere, darling," he answered taking in the show of pretty knees and the glimpse of lace peeping beneath her overall. George winked at Val telling her confidentially,

"We've got trouble here Val. First day and flirting

already."

"Are you bragging or complaining, George?" The man's eyes lit up in fake anticipation and began to paw the ground.

"Forget it George. She's only a baby," Val dampened his enthusiasm and went into the office. Winnie was waiting for a new parcel of needles to come up from the plating shop and she came over to Val reading the Indicator.

"Listen to this Val," and started reading,

There is a grave across the ocean
Where a brave young soldier sleeps
There is a dear old home in England
Where his wife often weeps
But peaceful be your sleep dear Sam
Tis sweet to breathe your name
In life I loved you dearly
In death I'll do the same
I think of him in silence
His name I oft recall
But there's no one left to answer
But his photo on the wall.

"Only 23 years old Val. This will be a dreadful situation, just think, we've lost the cream of our young population." Val went sorting the needles, but she thought of poor Fred her brother, still out there, and she agreed with Winnie.

"My brother is with the engineers. I'll be glad to see him home. Such a massacre. Such crass mistakes makes my blood run cold. I read yesterday that we have a brave army of lions led by donkeys. Thank them at the Crown Winnie when you pop in. Fred said he had received a parcel from them." Looking around the shop Val changed the subject and said,

"Where's Audrey today?"

"They say her Dora has diptheria."

"Not the baby? Our Mary went to her house last night to take her some apples." Another black dread loomed.

"Yes young Dora, her lives in Bridge Street by the station. Her mother and sisters are nursing her. Dr. Burns says the fever will reach a pitch today. I should take Mary up Worcester Road just in case there is a risk."

"I will tonight, Win. · As if we haven't enough to worry about." Val bent over her work, her face dull with anxiety. A few minutes later Mary Bourne arrived breathless, she said her daily bicycle ride into town every day from Hanbury kept her fit.

"Fit to drop," thought Val as she looked at Mary's overblown cheeks.

"What happened Mary? Not like you to be late."

"My mam's not very well. Her's got arthritis. Yesterday her scrubbed all over the great hall at Ragley. Now her knees are swollen. They only pay her sixpence. My mam was resting against the bannister when Milady trips by,

"What's the matter, my dear?" she asked my mam and my mam told her that her back was playing her up.

"Oh, we'll have to see about giving you a holiday." Her has got no intentions of giving a holiday to the staff. Her couldn't care less. Now today my mam had to get up early to pluck the chickens for Stratford market. She's got a few plums to sell, but she'll have to walk there and back 'cos they wants the use of the pony and trap at the Hall." Mary went off to get some work. The packing department was a much better place to work for the crude benches were covered in brown paper, the windows larger and cleaner. It was fairly free from pollution as the heavy machinery was downstairs. Val knew Mary Bourne's mother. The dominant image was of a 'rough diamond' class, and it was her violent defiant nature that fascinated Val. Mrs. Bourne loved washing clothes and tackled it like a steam roller. Since Val had started work Emmie Bourne had taken on the job of laundering the sheets and towels from Keepers Cottage. Last Monday evening when Val called for the laundry parcel, the cottage as usual was in applie pie order with the jerry pot on the table, full of milk, of course, it was a brand new pot, but she said this was easier to place under the goat. The whole set up characterized the occupier. A neglected lamb was squat on the hearth and she was nursing a piglet. She had been married twice, one had died at the beginning of the war and the second was killed while riding his bicycle home from work, so she had had her share of heart breaks, which probably produced her hard bitten outlook on life. Her second son, they said, had been born to a local grocer who had bought the cottage she now lived in. Rough, coarse, foul tongued, but fighting courageously against all odds. The roughness could be called honesty, but Val saw she tackled more work than any man.

There were animals all over the yard, three or four children, Val was never quite sure which were her own or other waifs and strays. She would gather them under her wing like a broody hen. Having all the virtues except virtue itself. Although Val was relieved to escape the harsh tongue, she admired the fighting spirit of the woman. Mary Bourne luckily did not inherit her mother's temper, although born and bred in that atmosphere there was no escape from the choice sayings her mother used out of habit, some of these stayed with the girl, but she did try to improve her speech and habits in a more refined way.

Mary was courting a nice lad from Tongue's farm. Each evening he would call with a few flowers or some sweets.

"He's bloody saaft in th' 'ead. Why doon't 'e bring some eggs or a piece of fat bacon, more like. He's a saaft big lump. Make sure you does that ironing, Mary, afore yer goos gum-suckin," her mother shouted.

"Alright, mam. Don't shout all the village will hear you."

"A lot I cares for them lot. All kippers and curtains."

"Well I'm still seeing Jimmy, he's well mannered and wants to get married."

"He'd better, after all this time, or he'll have me after him. You can tell him from me if he takes advantage of you I'll have his guts for garters." Luckily Mary survived the usual tirade and went on courting Jimmy, although his well meaning bouquet usually finished at the back of the fire. When Mary came back Val asked her,

"Did you go out last night, Mary?"

"Yes. We went a walk to Bentley. But my mam made me do the ironing first."

"Jimmy's prospects look good. How long have you been courting now?"

"It's nearly two years. We're getting engaged on Saturday. We're getting the ring from Hopkins in Evesham Street. He's not one much for saying fancy things, but he said the french girls had learnt him how to kiss. Honest Val, I forget everything and everybody. Of course, when he starts breathing hard I have to remind him of my mam and he soon simmers down. But he's lovely. I'll be glad to be lawful wed Val. I has to stop thinking about it 'cos I gets too excited."

"By springtime you'll have enough saved to get your wedding dress. I might be able to help you there as I haven't got much on the sewing machine at the moment. Yes, an Easter wedding would be grand and you'll look adorable. At least you've got the farm cottage to move into."

"He's quite a good hand at carpentry. He's started making our bed. No fancy sculpturing, but it's strong. That's the important thing. I've heard the women say here 'if the bedroom's right, the rest of the house is right.' You've got a good head on your shoulders Val. I wish my mom had your sense. She works hard, but she wastes the

44

money Val. She's too generous. She'd give her arse away and shit through her side, as they say. But she's promised to give us a good send off at the wedding."

"She's a worker Mary, and loves you so much. Try and please her. She shouts, but she means well," Val said trying to pacify the young girl. Mary was left to recover the work bench while Val went off to find Mr. Sisom, the boss, about the new work schedule.

Her mind was a mixture of religious emotion and political ideas as she saw the unfairness in a system which produced women like Emmie Bourne who had to lose their natural womanhood in order to cope with the demands of making ends meet. Mr. Sisom seemed genuine when he told Val that events were in progress that would ease a woman's burden, especially as there would be so many young widows after the war. He said his own mother had died in childbirth and he had vowed then, as soon as circumstances allowed, he would provide better facilities for the town hospital. The office was comparatively quiet and it gave Val the opportunity to tell of the conditions in the yard in Edward Street.

"It's so unhealthy, they're crammed in like salted fish in a barrel. Two toilets to six houses. The women try to keep them well scrubbed with boiling Soda water and there's always the square of neatly-cut newspaper strung together, but there's no dignity, no privacy, and when the drains overflow after a storm the stench is nobody's business. I don't know why that dirt cart cannot come round more often." Val knew she had a sympathetic ear and went on earnestly,

"Even Winnie, she lives in Catherines Place, says it's not much better. They have to take turns to do the dollying in the brew-house. It's near the shops and the chapel but there is too much congestion, they all have large families. It's almost impossible to live decently with such meagre facilities. Winnie's husband earns a few bob by cutting the workers' hair. Anybody can go to number five and get a short back and sides for two pence! 'It all helps,' Winnie says. But even with these few shillings extra they are only able to buy the bare necessities. There should be some form of unemployment pay, even to cover food and fuel. The poverty of these people are like two parts of the same nation. We're all God's children and these conditions should be made known publicly. Mind you, Mr. Sisom, there is no one as proud and industrious as the people of our town. No wonder they call some roads here nothing but kippers and curtains, and they should be admired for their pride." Val really voiced her opinion, she felt so strongly of the hard slog of these women-folk.

"You have the right idea Val. You should go in for politics. You seem to know all the answers. Thinking of joining this new Liberal Party myself. I'm sure I can count on your support now I see your point of view. We'll make it a better world between us Val. At least several measures have been extended in the scope of the National Insurance Scheme and that will deal with genuine unemployment. Of course, Val there are some who don't want work."

"No doubt, that's due to the unsettling effects of the war. The scars of blood, sweat and tears have given lasting nightmares for some of the returned soldiers. They see no incentive in the dreary aspect of going from bed to work."

"I must tell you Val, the scene is improving in housing. The Addison Act took into the central government housing for the first time. All local authorities are to state what houses are needed to make up the leeway caused by the war. So I see a future that holds promise, with better quality dwellings complete with enough space, bathrooms and water closets. That surely spells better hygiene for the people."

"Well it will certainly provide some dignity, which is everyone's right surely." And looking at the clock face said, "I'd better do some needle-packing, but it's so refreshing to talk to someone like you Mr. Sisom who realizes the needs and cares of his work force."

"You speak a lot of sense my dear," he handed over a sheaf of papers. "Will you chase these orders Val? Then come to the office, we'll have a cup of coffee." Estelle worked in the office, a tall, willowy, graceful girl in her late twenties and as Val passed the outer door of her office a noise of snuffling caused her to stare through into the small time-keeping place and Estelle was buried deep on the desk, sobbing uncontrollably. Val who was also concerned with the women's welfare at the factory felt it a duty to enquire the reason.

"I've left him Val" the girl said through swollen lips. It's impossible." Val comforted her caringly. There had never been close communication, for the girl always seemed so aloof and superior. Admitted, Val thought, her clothes sense is perfection, for she belonged to that type of person that seemed impossible to have ever undergone the wanton experience of the bedroom. Never a hair out of place. Apart from that, there was a particular sweet wholesomeness, as if her personality had been produced by parents who were very much in love.

"It will blow over Estelle" Val said.

"No, this is the finish, although I love him so much. It's jealousy. I can't bear to think of him talking or touching anyone else. But I can't bear this life any longer. My mother says he plays on my love for him. It's pure agony Mrs. Thomas. I realize that marriage is made up of a lot of little things, and it only needs one tiny displeasure to set off a tornado, but this is the ultimate blow."

"What of Alice and Johnny?"

"They are with my mother. They love him and I will never alienate their feelings. He's their father, after all. The quarrels are horrendous and my nerves won't stand it any longer."

"Life is dreadful alone Estelle. You don't realize how vulnerable you are, a woman on her own."

"I've thought it well over. Anything must be better than this torture. At least I'll have peace of mind if I can find a cottage on my own or some rooms."

"I know of two rooms going. It's not far away in Beoley Road if you are completely certain."

"Yes Mrs. Thomas my mind is made up."

"What happened?" Val thought by unburdening her worries there may be a happier solution.

"It's a series of many things. But as you know it was a beautiful summer's day last Saturday. The children arranged to go to a fete with my mother so I cherished the idea of a lovely day with John in the country. So I got up early, it would be heavenly around Bradley Green, I thought and I cooked some cornish pasties and a fruit cake intending to make a long day and enjoy our meals in the fresh air. It was going to be glorious just the two of us. Coming up to nine and my parents had collected the children. They were all neat and tidy in their best clothes. Alice wouldn't have a cooked breakfast but Johnny cleared his plate of bacon and egg and fried bread and after I'd cleared all the crocks away and packed the picnic in the cycle basket, the radio forecast gave out news of a fine summer's day. I watched them pelt up the path to get in the trap. Then I shouted up to John asking if he wanted breakfast. He didn't answer so I went upstairs thrilled with the surprise I was about to spring on him. He brushed by me quickly and I noticed he had on his best grey striped suit. That wouldn't be ideal for cycling. I followed him into the bathroom and he began clipping his moustache. I wondered what all this was about. On that, there was a knocking at the door. John turned his smiling face to me and announced,

"Oh that's George. We're going to Portsmouth for

a few days holiday." Seeing my displeasure he shouted,
"It's my holiday."

"That's it Mrs. Thomas, my heart is broken." Val felt
deeply at the girl's disappointment and promised to give her
any help she needed.

"Thanks Mrs. Thomas. I really need your common
sense. Please tell me the best thing to do," the girl pleaded.

"There are many generous souls in this factory Estelle.
Please try not to worry. We'll all help you." At last the girl
seemed more relaxed and Val sought an answer in the quiet
of her own office.

Estelle's words still ringing in her ears, "I want a lover
not a lecher."

CHAPTER EIGHT

BOB SEALEY

The house was unusually silent when Bob called on Val the following week. Through the kitchen window he could see a stream of light coming from under the sitting room door and, guessing she was at the machine let himself in, picking up the Indicator and sitting himself down near the fire deciding to wait for Val to make an appearance.

The house seemed ghastly without the children's noisy repartee. It was too early for them all to be in bed and he was mystified at the silence. Within the framework of his nature he loved Val but was hurt and estranged at her unresponsive attitude to his eager offer of support. For him it had been enough to keep her company, merely exist to ensure her well being, and know there was appreciation. But the weeks became months, the months, years, and although there seemed some real promise in her answer, "We'll see," Bob now felt the need of definite reassurance.

He found great difficulty in standing by, watching her daily struggle seeing her dear face age with stress and over-work. The fact that she seldom complained but soldiered on bravely, made it even harder to bear. Nevertheless, he expected an answer soon and his mind was made up; when she appeared, he had resolved to make a definite approach.

It seemed ages as he sat meditating, but when the hushed house did breathe life, and the sitting room door opened it wasn't Val that appeared but a young, singing girl. It was Joanne. Bob rose awkwardly and said slowly,

"Hello, I don't know you do I? Come to see Val. Where are they all? I've never known this house so quiet. I'll light the gas." He struck a match and put it to the gas mantle. She moved the kitchen chair saying,

"I'll help you." The faint smile upon her lips could have been derision, as the match petered out and nearly burnt his fingers. They laughed together at the catastrophe. Joanne held his hand steady at the second attempt. Bob sensed the sweet perfume of her hair so close to his face, as,

again he held the light to the fragile lace like tube.   The
peculiar yellow flame gave a radiance to her upturned face.
For a split second he read the invitation and immediately,
almost clumsily moved the massive kitchen table between
them, going to the window saying,
"I think I can hear Val coming."
"She won't be back yet.   She's gone over to Mrs.
Edwards to take some repaired curtains.   She asked me to
stay with the children for an hour.   Mary's gone over to
Ethel's house.   I was just looking at these old photographs.
Just look at Val's old fashioned dress here on her wedding
day."   Seeing his slight limp she asked,
"What's happened to your leg?   Is that the reason why
you are not away fighting?   Rejected on medical grounds?"
The forthright young lady shot out the questions with rather
nauseating precocity.   Bob leant against the dresser somewhat staggered by the barrage of blunt unsympathetic
questions.
"Yes. I had an accident a few years ago." Bob replied.
"I'm a freak," he went on with an unusual display of scornful
self pity.
"Nonsense, soothed the young girl."   He made as if to
go, but she would have none of it.   Aware of his self con-
sciousness, her smile now became mischievous,
"Oh, please don't go.   You cannot go without some
supper.   Val would never forgive me."   At this gentle
persuasion Bob sat at the table sorting out the faded photographs.   His face was grave and although now cool and self
controlled he whispered to himself, 'This is a dreadful state
of affairs.   This is definitely not the scene I had envisaged.'
With a masculine constriction of lips and jaw he said out
aloud,
"I'll stay awhile.   If she's not back soon, I'll come over
tomorrow night."   He felt it would be cowardly to leave on
impulse, but under the callous searching gaze of the
immature young lady he knew a wretched embarrassment.
She seemed to delight in his discomfort and placed her hand
around his neck as she reached up to the dresser-shelf for
cups and plates for supper.
"Don't get upset.   Val won't be long," she sighed.
"She's lucky to have such a strong handsome caller.   Why
don't you get married?   Despite her age, she is still quite
good looking?"
Bob, inwardly tortured with impatience, quaked at such
brazen   familiarity   and   wondered   how   Val   had   ever
befriended this girl.   He wrongly thought Val would not be
very pleased to come home and find this scene, so plucking

up courage decided it would be wiser to leave when the right moment presented itself. His exit might have to be abrupt, but he knew it would be a wise decision. Therefore, while Joanne departed into the back kitchen to bring in the milk, Bob, for all his disability made a hasty exit. The next thing Joanne heard was the pony and trap moving out of the yard.

"Ridiculous man. No patience. No wonder he's courting a woman old enough to be his mother," she said maliciously under her breath. At the height of her vicious imaginings, she heard Val opening the back door who, with an anxious look on her face, she asked Joanne about the children. Joanne was still laying the table, and told Val she had not heard a sound from them. Val was breathless from the ceaseless thrust of the October wind and went before the fire gladly. Joanne couldn't wait to explain,

"You had a visitor, Val. Bob Sealey. He's quite a dish."

"He's an old friend. The boys get on well with him. Have they been quiet? Thanks for coming over Joanne. Mary will be back on Sunday. Our Ethel isn't very well at all. I expect it's the new influenza germ. Hope Mary don't take it although I've dosed her well with quinnine. She's got a strong constitution. We'll have some supper, Jo then we'll be off to bed. I've put a hot water bottle in our Mary's bed for you." Joanne was not tired. Curiosity was the spur of the moment. The blonde beauty faced Val, bold to the point of recklessness as she informed her,

"Your chap's very serious Val. Nearly in tears when I mentioned his bad leg. I don't think he likes me. Just disappeared. No goodnight. No nothing," but Val assured her,

"He's a good lad. You'll soon be friends."

CHAPTER NINE

BY INDUSTRY FLOURISH

George Manders, the foreman must have noticed that Val was not wholly suited to the tasks in the polluted area of the machine shop, so the next Monday he told her Carrie Troth had left from the packing department to have a baby. Val could replace the vacancy. It was cleaner and less noisy. There was an amount of paper work, but Val's quick brain soon mastered this as a matter of course.

She was pleased with the transfer, but missed the boisterous company of the work force. Occasionally there was a visit made to hand out the order cards to the workers when, again, she would be informed of all the latest news. They thought her 'stuck up' since the transfer, but Val assured Phil Clements this was not the case giving out an invitation to Phil and Joanne to come over to the cottage for supper any evening.

"Our Mary starts here at the end of November, Phil. Keep an eye on her. Don't let her get put on. She's not very old. No doubt, before long she will get used to all the gossip and the leg pulling."

"Don't fret kid, she'll be fine. You knows her'll be alright with us," laughed Phil, followed by the usual,

"Does yer know, kid? They's gan the Germans 72 hours to sign the armistice."

"Well informed as ever, Phil. It would be wonderful. I heard on the radio that Marshall Foch has been handed the terms of the agreement. They are obliged to accept or reject it within that time, but I believe the Germans are so devastated and desperate they will be glad to accept at once.

We shall be counting the hours over this weekend, it should be signed by Sunday. What joy to be back to normal living once more, but Mr. Sisom is wondering where the returning soldiers will find employment. I suppose now the women have served a purpose they will be pushed out," Val waged.

"There's one consolation in our town, the work is light and fragile suitable for women. I expect they'll still find me some flys to dress. Anyway we'll have some peace and quiet. Some future to enjoy. Wait till I tell you this Val. My mom and Auntie Minnie went to stay the night at Auntie Bella's in Beoley Road. Well, I went round to see my mom this morning and 'er gan us a parcel. We couldn't see what was in it. Any road, when Auntie Bella was in the other room Auntie Minnie nervously explained how the buttons on the new flock bed tortured her back bone, so she sat up nearly all night cutting them off by candle light with a pair of nail scissors she had in her bag. Her handed over the parcel of buttons making us vow not to pass it on to Auntie Bella."

"Your Auntie Bella would have forty fits, and die in the first," she warned. "At lunch time I was talking to cousin Joe and he says his mam had threatened to take the new mattress back to the shop to complain as there were no buttons sewed on. I laughed 'til I wet myself Val." Val also vowed to keep quiet.

"I'd better not let on when I see Bella at Rice's shop at dinner time." Val heard Lizzie telling Edna Brough, "I see they're advertising for day and night shift workers doing shells at the Austin, Longbridge. They are offering accommodation as well, in a hostel. Who the bloody 'ell wants to live there? Anyway by Monday their advertisement will be wasted if the Jerries surrender." She asked Val as she passed close,

"Does yer like yer new job Val? Don't forget us here in the machine shop now you's gone up in the world." Val stopped to have a chat.

"Yes thanks Lizzie. Why don't you come to Keepers Cottage on Saturday night and we'll listen for the news on the radio. If it's good we'll have a celebration. Come with Phil and Joanne and you'll have company to walk back across the town."

"Alright Val, I will. If it's right with Joanne we'll be round about four o'clock. I's promised to get some lamp oil first from Dyers in Alcester Street. I see in the Indicator Dick James out of Walford Street has got in arrears with his wife's maintenance. He's got to pay her ten shillings a week." As Val made to move on called,

"See you Saturday, Val." Val hurried back to the cleaner atmosphere of the packing department. At least here she could hear herself think straight. Just seventy two hours. God send Fred home safe and sound, she prayed. Only a matter of hours, minutes, when the town could sleep soundly in bed at night. She asked herself fiercely, 'Why do men have to fight?'   Her boss Mr. Sisom wished her 'good day' and stopped to have a chat.

"I was just wondering Mr. Sisom, why do men always have to fight?" Val asked.

"Well Val, what is the alternative?   It's a case of offering the other cheek to bullies until it's sore," he shrewdly tried to explain.

"But surely there must be a more humane method of thinning out the population," Val sighed.   With calculated wisdom the man went on,

"My dear Val.   If you have some sensible plan tell this government.   The sheer waste of manhood is callous.   But if one is confronted by a bully so many times the stress is as frustrating as retaliation."

"As a mother I woud say take the softer way."

"You sound like a pacifist Val.   If we all took the softer way we would have the huns doing the goose step down Alcester Street at this very moment.   No one is immune in this lot.   My youngest brother died in hospital at the start of the war in the first week.   He was only eighteen.   At least we did have an opportunity of being with him at the end. Thousands have vanished into thin air.   Blown to smithereens.   This is the war to end all wars, Lloyd George informs us.   So when the mailed fist is unmailed perhaps we will have a government to see to it, and we shall never have to bear these atrocities ever again."

"But look at the price of things.   They say we shall soon have to pay ninepence for a loaf," Val sounded anxious.

"Do you think there will be mass unemployment?   If I lose this job, how could I possibly exist on a widow's pension?"

"Lloyd George has promised us a country fit for heroes to live in, and that there are already plans to lay foundations for a better society.   At the moment men are too preoccupied with winning the war.   That in itself is an overwhelming task and now the people are weary and even too exhausted to hope.   Even the government realizes war is senseless and wasteful, so they intend to create a League of Nations."

"Every mother would vote 'yes' to that," Val agreed.

"There is a blueprint for a better Britain.   New and better houses to rent for the poorer people with proper sanitation.   Abolish slums forever.   They have already raised the school leaving age to fourteen, also the beginning of day continuation schools to improve education.   Even working conditions are under review.   The Whitley Committee have recommended the creation of Joint Industrial Councils representing both employers and workers.   Wages and hours will be negotiated between government and local councils. Post war Britain will be a very different land to pre war Britain, Val. There is great talk of a Labour Party as a portent of the future. On social issues there will be reforms for the poor by radical matters of housing, unemployment relief and the like. They envisage public ownership of major industries, such as mines and railways."

"I don't truly understand the finer points of politics Mr. Sisom, but now we have the vote more women must gain by studying the whys and wherefores of any new government's proposals if Lloyd George retires. The suffragettes have proved their point, suffering long, hard arguments to gain the vote that only fools would ignore the power of a woman's initiative in the making of this brave new world they talk about."

"You are a strong character Val. We sorely need people of your strong instincts to form new and beneficial policies on housing, education and health. Half an hour of a woman's down to earth understanding is worth hours of rhetoric by some distant Member of Parliament miles away. Keep at it Val. You have some sound ideas. You may count on my support if you decide to stand for a council seat."

"Thanks Mr. Sisom, I get carried away when politics are mentioned, especially concerning children's welfare. Now I must get some work done or you will be reading the Riot Act. It seems this weekend will see a new destiny for us all," Val said as she reluctantly ended the interesting conversation. Inwardly she was seething at the thought of her precious sons being considered as cannon fodder to further the power of some unseen future politician. With a precious inborn foresight she envisaged a future where the work force would have the power to enforce the capitalists into a fairer distribution of profits. Remembering the poem by Crane from Bromsgrove that Bob had read to her last night.

"The seige of Redditch, I was there all the while,
With nothing to eat but a piece of tile.
Men, women and children with trade all alive;
Clods, pebbles and brickbats sent at us full drive.
Sent at us on purpose to batter our plates;
Tongs, shovels and pokers and cheeks of old grates;
A line of stout women, with ladles three deep,
Determined to drive us or send us to sleep.
The leader well armed with a stout wooden crutch,
Ten women to one Bromsgrove man, is too much.
The sun sunk away at the sight of the fun,

The moon at the brightest, to light us to run.
When quarrels are up to a terrible pitch,
Be off, like a crane, from the siege of Redditch.
I'm singing of sieges, your chance is but small,
The siege of Redditch is the flogger of all.

Val had read of injustices meted out to honest, industrious working people and vowed to show her compassion in a
practical way by canvassing for votes at the next election.

CHAPTER TEN

THE MAIL FIST UNMAILED

All that weekend the world waited for Germany's decision, but it didn't reach Redditch until nearly eleven o'clock on that November day in 1918. Within five minutes of the Armistice each factory and school was empty. They said 'as empty as the Crown Prince's head', Little Willie, they had nicknamed him.

Redditch celebrated at St. Stephen's Church which was packed to capacity and the hymns sung with sincere gusto. After the service Val, Bob Sellers, Phil, Joanne and Lizzie and the children went back to Keeper's Cottage for a meal. While the womenfolk prepared the table the boys gathered in some logs and after tea all joined in a sing song around the sitting room fire. Phil and Lizzie stayed the night and it was after ten when Val asked Bob to give Joanne a lift home.

The rejoicing was marred by the news that Clarry's younger brother Walter, only nineteen, had died in France of his wounds the same day the Armistice was signed. It was so painfully ironic. There was consolation in a letter from his Colonel saying he was the finest soldier in the regiment. Clarry was confused by emotion for days and Val felt heart-broken at her own utter helplessness.

The following Friday Val felt a deathly chill as Mary read out the verse from the Indicator:

"He marched away so bravely
His young head proudly held
His footsteps never faltered
His courage never failed
There on the field of battle
He calmly took his place
He died for England's honour
And the glory of his race
When the roll call is sounded up yonder
And the Saviour counts the brave
Our brother will be amongst them
For his life he nobly gave.

Val shed a tear as she prayed for the lad. Her heart went out to his poor mother and father and to Clarry who only this week had received a letter from him saying he was looking forward to coming home for Christmas. Mary continued to read telling her mother of how the authorities expected the young children to stand outside in the cold weather. Toddlers of four years old sent into the playground without overcoats.

"I suppose that is the Headmistress's way of hardening them. We are compelled to send them to school. It's up to the authorities to keep them warm. No wonder there's a spate of colds and toothache. I'm glad Clarry is willing to care for my Topsy at home. But I must make a trip to Bridge Street School before long to see if they can take her in the New Year. Oh, here's Clarry coming up the path. Open the door, Mary. You know it's knocked her about losing Walter." Clarry was soon in the house and took from her basket a small bag.

"I've been to Sanders. A small loaf each Val. The manager said there was only enough for the written orders. For the people from Birchfield Road who can afford large orders. No wonder the working class are getting disheartened." Mary was still reading from the newspaper and said to Clarry,

"Did you see this advertisement from Edward Dyer, Mrs. Bailey? Save six pence a day during the first year and then you can own your own home." Val piped in,

"I couldn't save sixpence a day Clarry. I'm still in debt for my machine and I really make good use of that. Mary has started work at Milwards in the workshop. George has promised me as soon as there's a place Mary can come into the packing department. Phil Clements has promised to watch she gets some decent jobs. Our boss is back from the war zone and I've heard through the grape vine he intends to visit the factory next week. I expect Mr. Sisom will retire when the other partner is back in harness." Clarry didn't stay long and after a quick cuppa said cheerio to Mary and Val walked a little way along the lane with her.

All that week the factory was agog with excitement, for the young handsome officer had promised new and better conditions for the work force. There was a much brighter atmosphere as they felt already a new surge of prosperity with the coming of peace. There would be overtime and wages would rise sharply as people bought many goods that they were unable to purchase during the war. The factory sparkled with a new vigour of hope for the future. On the day of the proposed visit Mary had a job quite close to Val's bench and she looked particularly sweet in an effort to impress the new boss. Janet had made her a silk blouse of a pale coral colour. It blended so harmoniously with her fair skin that Val felt understandably proud.

It was well into the morning when Phil saw the impressive car drive into the yard. Val estimated the age of the driver to be in the late twenties, early thirties. A fine man, somewhere over six feet in height with skin burnt bronze by the foreign sun and wind. His black hair was as thick as a boys. He looked up at the waiting girls and Val saw in the light blue eyes a sincere kindness such as is scarcely seen in army men. Mr. Sisom soon escorted him through the processes of the needle making, polishing and finishing. When he eventually returned to the office via the packing department his eyes again shone with a genuine kindness as he watched Mary making the tea. The girl was shyly clumsy but with a quiet dignity he steadied the cup for her and said paternally,

"Like this, my dear." Mary glowed with surprise as he queried,

"And what is your name little Miss Pretty?" Mary told him and without more ado he had vanished into the rambling office beyond the packing department. Val was curious as to the questions raised, but Mary with youth's indifference said,

"I can't remember. Oh, he only asked me my name," changing the subject, "What time do we finish today mam? I'm going with Pam, Phil Clements girl to the Picture House to see 'A self made lady'. I'll have tea at their house and Pam's brother Martin said he would see me home on his bike." Val felt an anti climax to the excitement of the day. Looking through the window she saw Harry's father crossing the yard. He looked up and Val wished he would stop awhile. There would be so much knowledge he could impart. That intelligent bearing of face and figure gave every appearance of sense and stability. She longed to hear his private thoughts and ideas. But he never stopped and Val realized how lucky she was to still have Bob's company. His rustic humour always raised her from the doldrums of the daily round, the common task. At six o'clock the hooter, silent for many years, sounded knocking off time, and there was the usual dash for coats, scarves and bags. The day that had begun so well now turned into sadness for Phil told Val that Audrey's little girl had died about midday.

CHAPTER ELEVEN

CHRISTMAS AT KEEPERS COTTAGE

Soon at the factory it was pudding week, when every-one on the shop floor worked to extent, this was the week before the holiday when the workers needed a fat wage packet. With the extra cash they were able to have pudding as well as a dinner. The icing on the cake, as it were. Val had filled the cupboards with jams and jellies, pickled vege-tables and bottled fruits from the orchard. Early in the year Bob had successfully set some goose eggs under a broody hen from which appeared two plum goslings. They should be quite fully grown for Christmas.

Sacks of potatoes and strings of onions filled the store shed. It was Saturday, Bob had taken the boys to the Palace to see Lockharts' famous elephants trained by Captain Taylor.

This left Val and Mary free to wrap and store the gifts in suitable hiding places until the great day. Coal was still in short supply, only a month's supply could be ordered, but Tom's brother had arranged to bring a load well in time for winter, and Bob had seen to it that yule logs were plentiful.

Christmas Day that year fell on the Wednesday and Val was up well before the boys' voices could be heard. A great gleam soon set the room ablaze as Val lit the neat pile of sticks and coal prepared by Bob the previous night. The brew house fire was still smouldering, so more dry twigs were added to coax it into the furnace needed for the day's heavy cooking.

Still in their night clothes, Edward and Tom came tumbling downstairs clutching their goodies. Edward proudly presented his wooden engine to his mother for inspection and praise, and Val then requested Tom to display the brightly coloured scrap book.

"Now play quietly by the fire. Don't disturb Topsy or I'll never get a thing done."

"She's awake," said Edward, "I heard her talking to

Mary." On that Mary shouted down to her mother,

"We're coming." Tom straightened a silver ball that slanted too close to the wall in danger of falling from the decorated pine tree. He was a perfectionist.

Mary carried her young sister close to her mother for a kiss. Topsy's chubby face looked rosy and wrinkled on the side where she had slept. She closed the enormous blue eyes and snuggled into Mary's shoulder not quite wide awake.

"See what Father Christmas has brought her mam," Mary said, trying to coax the baby awake by tickling her bare tummy and at last the pearly teeth showed in a baby grin. Her tiny face became radiant as she saw the Christmas tree decorated with sugar mice and piglets, the more garish ornaments shining brilliantly in the firelight. Val asked Mary if she had unwrapped her own present and out came a gush of pleasure as she answered,

"Yes, mother, it's lovely. Wherever did you get it? My favourite blue and it fits perfectly. I don't remember you taking my measurements." Val smiled, knowing her secret had kept well.

"Ha, ha, you don't know everything young lady." The response was no more than a whisper as Mary hugged and kissed her mother.

"I love you, our mam." Edward was flat on the floor running the engine over the most level part of the sitting room floor. Tom was already pasting in his favourite puppy pictures in his scrap book. The second Christmas without Alf. Val brushed away the sad memories as she indulged in a brief enjoyment of the charming scene. A general giggle fluttered from one to another. Minutes passed. Whispers were exchanged and Val prayed they would remain in harmony for a while, although with their healthy schoolboy vitality this was too much to expect. Val hurriedly prepared breakfast trying desperately to hide the dampness on her cheeks.

"Please look after Topsy Ed while I help mam to lay the table," Mary pleaded. Sorting out the pantry Val told Mary,

"Mrs. Edwards sent us a pot of pork dripping Mary. Smells delicious. Look at the jelly at the bottom of the jar. We can use that for breakfast." The thick crusts of toast and peppered dripping were soon demolished by the boys so that their new toys would not be too neglected.

"We'll have some porridge Mary, and the bab can have her bread and milk," Val declared. Steam soon saturated the out house as the puddings boiled merrily and Val began to organise the dinner menu. Mary sang Baby Baby Buntin', daddy's gone a huntin, while she struggled to get the bodice over the little girl's head.

"Now put your dolly down one minute while I put on your petticoat, our bab."

"It's too tight, you're hurting me Mary," protested Topsy.

"Never. There, I said it would only take a minute." When she had dressed Topsy and brushed the bright curls into order Topsy said,

"I want to whisper something." Mary, puzzled, bent her head down and listened intently to the whispering of the sweet rosebud mouth.

"I love you Mary."

"I love you too Topsy. Now sit quietly in your chair otherwise we will never have any dinner today." Val came bustling in from the yard carrying a big basket of russet apples.

"You boys will have to get from under my feet. Get yourselves dressed and take these parcels to Clarry Bailey. They are only small items for the young ones, but they are all I can afford. You can stay awhile, but don't get in Mrs. Bailey's way. Bob is bringing his mother over after dinner," Val promised them.

"Hurrah, hurrah," shouted Tom and Edward together. A great deal of preparation had been dealt with the previous night and already the aroma of roast goose filled with sage and onions gave off that unique appetising Christmas smell.

Into mid morning apples were popping as they simmered on the hob. Val asked Mary to take Bob and Mrs. Sealey their presents begging her not to be away too long. Mary rarely disposed to grumble remarked on all the work still to be done, but Val convinced her that there was still plenty of time, so she agreed, promising to return immediately.

Val went on ceaselessly loading the table with plates, cutlery, fruit and holly until a sharp back pain made her wince. 'Five minutes won't hurt' she thought, so putting up her feet on the day bed did a quick recap of the meal.

She had cooked the ham overnight which was in the meat safe, now cold and ready to carve. Bob would help her to carve that for high tea; and Tom had fetched the game pie that was Mrs. Edwards's annual gift. Tom had said that, at Mrs. Edwards's query as to their needs, he assured here that the geese had grown well, and that as Val was now working, this year there would be a better holiday. Val had warmed at the thought of such unselfish kindness.

Usually for Christmas tea, Val, after most of the heavy chores were over, wore a new blouse or jersey, but this year's budget really did not run to new clothes for herself, so she had already decided she must make do with the pink silk blouse that had already seen several Christmases. She told herself sharply, food and gifts came before vanity, and dismissed the thought and murmured,

"We can't have everything. Thank God for the things we have. Peace, love and happiness." Having allowed herself a few minutes musing over the last twelve months she realized her good fortune; especially the news that Fred and Bill her brother-in-law were well on their way home. With these prayers answered she found a renewed strength and deliberately put all sad thoughts away and went to the window staring anxiously up the lane. Yes, there they were coming charging down the lane, Tom shouting, Gee up! gee up! while Edward pretending to be in the shafts galloped sideways avoiding the ice covered pot holes. Fortunately dinner was well on the way and Val had the opportunity to discuss the exchange of presents from Mrs. Bailey before Mary returned. A while after, Mary appeared on the door-step carrying a large mysterious parcel. Edward rushed to the door excitedly shouting,

"What's in there, what's in there?"

"Give me chance to get in," Mary cried. As Val attended the basting of the roast goose she heard gasps of delight,

"Mine's a clown," Edward declared.

"Mine's a box of marbles. Come on Ed let's have a quick game before dinner." They cleared off into the sitting room too engrossed in who should take first shot to see Mary hand over Mrs. Sealey's present to Val.

"Here's a towel mam. First wipe your hands well. Bob's mother said she hoped you'd like it."

"You open it for me love while I keep the gravy stirred." Mary let the wrappings fall slower and slower smiling teasingly at her mother. At last folds of mint green satin fell onto the table as the parcel spilled its contents. Val forgot the chores and wiped her hands thoroughly asking Mary,

"I wonder what it is? What a divine colour. A gorgeous blouse, Mary. Isn't she good? That's just the idea. She's a gem.

"Yes it will please Mrs. Sealey if you wear it tonight."

"I haven't had anything new for ages." As the lovely satin garment was unfolded Val gasped,

"Just look at the panels of lace and the gigot sleeves and the stiff high collar," Val enthused.

"Yes it should suit you admirably. It's smart the way

these dainty self covered buttons decorate the cuffs and the neck. I'm dying to see you wearing it. I'll hang it up in your bedroom ready for tonight." As she gathered up the garment delicately Val murmured,

"Oh, well. If He doesn't come He sends. That's another seasonal wish answered," and called after the disappearing girl,

"What time are they coming over?"

"She said about four, if that's alright," Mary called back.

"Yes we'll have time to make some mince pies and get some good fires going by then," Val said under her breath. When Mary returned Val enquired if Mrs. Sealey's chilblains were easier.

"She never mentioned them, but I could smell Zambuck ointment."

"She's as tough as a bone, remarkable woman. Did Bob like his pullover?"

"Very much. He was laughing as he said he'd be brave and wear it tea time." Val smiled as she snapped, "Cheek of it" in mock severity. She remembered his teasing banter as he remarked on the colour while she was making it.

"Looks like goose-turd green," he had teased Val.

"That's a nice thing to say. It's a lovely sage green."

"I'm only pulling your leg gal. It's wizard. Your clever fingers could turn a sugar bag into a thing of fashion."

"Now then Bob. None of the sob stuff," she remembered telling him.

When Topsy awoke she seemed peevish, so Edward showed her the new scrap book and the display of kittens and lambs set out on the first page, which soon had her smiling and chattering. Tom and Mary were like busy bees making the living room a hive of activity, filling the already overloaded table with extras, nuts and sweets. Val gave Edward a smacker under the mistletoe as she passed by en route to the back kitchen, then pushed a morsel of Cadbury's chocolate in Topsy's mouth.

The blight of poverty and sadness was completely alien today, and as the kitchen's commotion slackened and the quondam steamed room cleared, Val relaxed and her face showed an unworried happiness. The bird sat magnificently on the table. Before the happy, hungry children began dinner Tom was allowed to say grace. There was a world of thankful gratitude and joy as she whispered 'Amen'. They did full justice to the meal. Sizzling crispy roast potatoes, kidney beans salted away in the autumn and frost-flavoured Brussels sprouts and the well gravied meat of the goose disappeared as if by magic. Mary helped to cut up Topsy's meat, while no sound came from Edward or Tom as they tucked in manfully and for a short time only the crackle of the log falling into place disturbed the vacuum.

Soon the smell of the richly spiced pudding wafted into the living room and Tom licked his lips in anticipation. Val had poured over a drop of brandy, a new luxury for this home and there were cheers as she carried it into the room complete with traditional scarlet berried holly.

"Can we have some burnt raisins like dad used to make for us?" asked Edward.

"After you've eaten your pudding. But keep quite still or there may be an accident. I'll do it Mary. This job needs caution." And so to finish the truly festive meal a dish of brandy soaked raisins were set alight while the eager fingers suffered the blaze to secure the juicy fruit. The boys were ushered into the sitting room and when the table had been completely cleared and the fire replenished, Val heard Mary calling her to come quickly into the sitting room. There Mary pointed to the miniature cane chair in the corner.

"Look mam at Topsy, she's fast asleep." The baby's head was leaning back against the bare wall, her podgy fingers clutching the new peg doll. Val with some concern said,

"I'll get a cushion to place behind her head. I wish I could creep into a corner and go to sleep," Val joked.

"You can now. Come on. Into that armchair. No ifs or buts. Put your feet up our mam. The visitors won't be here for a couple of hours."

"But I've got to turn out the jelly for the trifle," Val protested.

"You stay there," Mary ordered as she kissed her mother's cheek.

"Righto then if you insist," said Val sinking into the armchair. Mary placed her finger to her lips in an endeavour to hush the two boys, and Val happily closed her eyes. About an hour later she rose and said to Mary,

"That was heaven." In the feeble light of a dull fire she stared around the room as a traveller searches for familiar landmarks.

"Where's the boys?"

"They've gone up to the farm. We need more milk. They should be back soon."

Val looked from the sitting room window, no sign of the 'milkmen'. The sky was yellow as if holding a wealth of snow. The fuchsias still hung with buds like hanging jewels, but the remaining spears of golden rod were limp from last night's severe frost.

Mary peered tenderly at Topsy still in a contented slumber in her pram and suggested,

"We've got some time mam. Come on I'll dress your hair." Val agreed to be spoiled for once and Mary made an expert job of coiling, plaiting and coaxing the side tendrils of her mother's hair until Val cried in desperation, not used to such luxury.

"Hurry up Mary. That will do. They'll be here directly."

"Don't worry. There. Now have a look in the mirror, you look like a princess," said Mary triumphantly, happy to show her expertise. Val stood gazing wonderingly into the full length mirror. The deep auburn hair taken well back from her face hung in thick coils and the girl had really gone to extreme fashion and intertwined a pearl necklace through the copper coloured locks. Val couldn't believe what she saw. To be truly robust the figure could have been somewhat plumper, but by Mary's love and devotion all the worry lines and furrows had disappeared from her brow. The panels of rich lace against the spring green satin made a perfect match with the olive green velvet skirt of yesteryear.

Mary gave a last pat and said,

"You'll do, our mam."

"Bob won't know me," Val said and she laughed as coming down to earth she breathed,

"I wonder how long this coiffure would last on washing day."

"Never mind washing day. You look adorable now. Enjoy tonight," and hearing noises went quickly to the window, made for the door.

"That's them now mam. Come on, let's welcome our visitors in style for once." Bob was giving his mother a hand down when Val and Mary appeared at the door. When Bob turned to greet the hostess, he stood back unbelievingly.

"We have come to the wrong house mother. Who are these two apparitions? Did you ever see a lovelier picture?" Bob joked.

'Ha" said Mrs. Sealey, "the blouse fitted and the colour suits you. Bob chose it. He's familiar with your colour scheme. You have the right slim waistline for the new waisted styles. My waist went to pot years ago." Florrie said.

"Do come in. You are most welcome. And thanks for my superb present," and as Bob kissed her cheek she observed, "And you were brave to wear your new jersey."

"I needed it Val. It's warm and practical, and more precious, you made it with your own fair hands," he bragged.

They were divested of their outdoor clothes and led into the warm sitting room.

"Bob tells me you are coping quite well on your own Val. You are a brave girl," Florrie Sealey told her sincerely.

"With the rigours of making the home comfortable and the livestock protected there isn't time to fret. The important thing is to keep on top of the work, which with God's help and Bob's I have managed to do," Val told her. The house was hushed, so they made a solemn group and Bob enquired after the youngsters.

"It's unnaturally quiet, where are they all?"

"Don't speak too soon. They were alive at an unearthly hour. It's a wonder they didn't hear you coming along the drive. Mary's gone to change. Topsy as you can see is 'out' to the world and the two boys have slipped up to the farm for milk," Val explained and went on, "Clarry's family are coming over to tea, so we'll enjoy the quiet before the storm. I'll make a cuppa. The kettle is boiling."

"It always is," said Bob. "I'll make it. You two have a well earned rest."

"Mary has spoiled me rotten today. Anyone would think I was an invalid, but I do appreciate it. Love is so comforting," Val told Florrie. Bob shouted from the living room,

"It's snowing." He touched the fire with the black fire iron, and the pile of slack that was heaped behind the burning logs fell forward into the furnace causing a brilliant blaze that illuminated every corner of the room. He held his numbed fingers before the bars glad to be indoors.

He carried the loaded tea tray into the sitting room consoling the two ladies,

"No more shortages, girls. No more queues. No more seeing our chaps mutilated and diseased. You know Stan Boulton, Val? They say he took a battering from the gas. It blew in the wrong direction. Perishing stuff. He will never be the same again."

"Now then, Bob," said his mother, "give the war a rest. It's holiday. We've come to bring cheer not depression." The thin old voice carried a warmth of affection even in chiding, but despite the warning Bob went on,

"Yes, a few months and we'll be back in routine." With that to digest and after swallowing a mug of tea, told the ladies that he would meet the boys half way. Val and Florrie indulged in the peace and quite a little longer.

"You've been busy, Val," Florrie said, observing the cupboards and shelves loaded with jams and pickles.

"Yes," said Val, "when I close my eyes in bed, there is

great pleasure in remembering each day's achievement. Work is the salt of life and my own mother's maxim; 'a job worth doing, is worth doing well'. It's not always feasible, but if you aim for a hundred per cent satisfaction it's enough to even reach ninety nine percent. That can't be bad. Bob's vitality has helped enormously, the boys adore him."

"Yes. It's said a good son, a good husband. I only had Bob, that was enough responsibility to shoulder alone. He never knew his father, he walked out on me years ago. I was much older than Robert, but my parents insisted on marriage when I became pregnant. That's a lifetime away. Life has been lonely but not pitiable. My music has filled my life and there are great rewards seeing a student give unequalled delight to the community on the strength of your teaching."

"Music is a language on its own. I understand that." Bob had never mentioned his definite intentions to his mother although he couldn't hide his feelings for Val completely and he had dropped a hint last week when he informed her casually that there might have to be a few changes made in the new year. Consequently Florrie was thrilled to receive the invitation to Keepers Cottage and witness herself the beauty and character of the young widow that took up a great deal of her son's time.

"I love Christmas, Val, especially Christmas tea. I was so pleased to get your invitation. I love company. Time's gone by I have been so desperate to share, that I've asked a body in off the street to enjoy our festive table."

"Your heart is as big as a bucket, Florrie, Bob's told me of your generous parcel and gifts to the soldiers at Hewell Grange."

"Bread thrown upon the waters, comes back threefold. I've proved that to be true. But what I do resent is to read Lord Rhondda calling us grumblers and grousers. If he had the necessity to leave the washing to go up to Sanders to queue for bread, he'd have good cause to grumble. These people are out of touch with reality. All this Liberal clap trap: Out of time and experience comes sympathy, out of sympathy, tact; out of tact, understanding; out of understanding, hope. Just so many words. These politicians just battle to prove a victor of memorable quotations. I'm so proud of the women who have struggled so staunchly to get us the vote. I'm determined to see my vote is used to advantage."

"Me, too," agreed Val.

With that their conversation came to an abrupt end for the boys burst into the room clutching their new gifts.

"It's snowing mam. It's snowing," shouted Edward

68

excitedly.

"Leave your boots in the out house, put your plimsoles on," shouted Val, worried lest the snow should scatter over the new rug.

"You've got a wonderful family, Val. One to be proud of."

"They are growing up too fast Florrie. I hate the thought of losing them. But as my friend Clarry says,

"They are only lent to us," but yes, I am proud of them." On that Edward asked,

"Can we go into the sitting room until tea is ready?"

"Yes, yes. Look after Topsy, Edward. I think she has just woken up. Give her this, but only a small piece at a time, mind," Val coaxed handing him a piece of sugar mouse.

The multi coloured lanterns on the decorated pine tree lit up the far corner of the sitting room and the blue, green and red patterns showed magically on the low ceiling. Bob brought in a supply of logs before he changed his shoes.

There was a rumpus at the back door. It was the whole Bailey family and their father forbade them to enter the cottage until they had sung some carols. Bob shouted good humouredly through the window,

"Not tonight thanks. They've already been." Val soon had them all indoors, the sight of them, singing, shouting, joking filled her with sweet pleasure. Putting a welcoming arm around Clarry's shoulders Val steered her into a comfortable armchair close to the sitting room fireplace, whispering in her ear,

"Happy Christmas Clarry."

"Thanks, Val. Same to you and your family." Clarry had helped her so unstintingly over the last arduous months and now Val could prove her deep appreciation.

There were bodies strewn across the floor, across the sofa and on any lap available. Sandy and Bluey the two smaller puppies had jumped into the basket out of the way, but Cindy the cat stretched luxuriously inside the fender.

"That cat will get burnt, one of these days our mam," warned Tom.

"No. I think she has a sixth sense. She knows how to move from danger. Just watch her go when the sparks fly," Bob told him. Florrie helped to prepare the table. She was well known for her dainty wafer thin slices of bread and butter. Mary piled up the mince pies on a doileyed plate. Val's creative artistic efforts were evident on the massive festive cake. It was impossible to obtain the perfect icing appearance due to shortage of necessary ingredients, nevertheless, the scarlet berries, silver balls and glace fruits presented quite a Christmas scene as it took pride of place in the table centre.

The boys had been taught before the holiday to produce paper bon bons, although no one was allowed to guess the tiny gifts hidden inside the wrapping until each guest had found the allotted place at table. Tom had arranged these suitable for each individual guest. The silver and gold on the amateur foldings shone merrily in the fire's gleam.

Val had covered the ham in breadcrumbs and had already given it an expert pattern of scored markings, and placed it on the small meat dish. The tongue had been taken from the press. Bowls of preserved fruits and collected hazel nuts and chestnuts for roasting were all brought forward to enhance the tea time display.

The menfolk were discussing the merits of the parsnip wine patiently uncorked by Bob. At last, 'to table' Val called. Florrie and Clarry were deciding on the main ingredient for a Christmas pudding.

"I always grate up a carrot, and together with a table-spoonful of black treacle, that produces that very dark, almost black mixture," Florrie advised. But Clarry would have her own superior method of 'A glass of old Liffey. That's what puts the body in a pudding." Val would not be drawn into the discussion and jokingly suggested there should be a tasting competition. But Mr. Bailey a true Irishman settled for the Liffey addition no matter what dish they were concocting. But, as Clarry said, 'he would, wouldn't he?"

Bob and James lifted the long sofa closer to the table piling it high with cushions so that all would be seated. Clarry's children, Michael, little James, and Robert would be comfortable on the sofa. Bridie would sit on her mother's lap, and Topsy on Val's lap while Bob carved up the meats, and Mary, Tom and Florrie handed the plates round.

Angela and John had gone to Hanbury to John's parents farm, Clarry told Val. Val and Clarry sat the young girls side by side on the rug while they carried in teapots and hot water jugs.

"Let Clarry be 'mother' Mary. It's absolutely scalding and that family teapot is too heavy for you." To have looked in on the scene no one would have guessed that a long, hellish war had prevailed a few weeks ago. They all joined in Val's prayer of thanksgiving for such a peaceful and victorious conclusion.

After such a huge dinner Val was surprised to see the boys tucking in with a hungry gusto, but soon there were protests of 'No more, I'm full. I'm full." Towards eight o'clock Bob was asked to tell them some horrible 'really frightening' ghost stories. This gave the women a chance of a good gossip over the table, clearing away the remains of the depleted meal.

"A lovely meal, Val. You've worked hard," said Clarry.

"Thanks Clarry. Lovely to see you all. A pity we can only afford it once a year," Val answered. James had his own special recipe for hot punch. No one was allowed to see the concoction he mixed in with the bubbling apple juice but with the spices and old ale it gave off an overwhelming aromatic whiff that Bob couldn't wait to taste the brew. No one noticed the snow drifting silently over the backyard.

There were toffees and chocolates passed round and round. Bob had to perform his competition of biting the apple. A fine juicy apple was hung from a cord and held high in the air while it swung to and fro tantalisingly near the open jaws. The reward was a mouthful of fruit and the cord was lowered accordingly for those lesser in stature. Bob saw to it that each one had a fair share before the game ended. Topsy rolled in glee at seeing all the goodies and all the laughing loving friends.

James warmed by the potent drink told tales his father had handed down, he related that one of the principle amusements of the town was bull baiting which took place in various parts of Redditch. One of the favourite localities was behind the tanhouse and in a meadow the Star and Garter public house at Crabbs Cross. A man was allocated to the job of looking to the interests of the bull and to see fair play.

Apparently a good bull dog made straight for the nose and if he caught in any other place would keep changing his grip until he got hold of the desired spot. But other dogs would rush at the nearest part, tail or nose being a matter of no importance. Often the dog would be sent by the bull whirling in the air and then all hands would rush to the rescue before he fell. Sometimes the bull would inflict terrible injuries on the dog, they said it was unusual to see a good dog with all his bones in their normal condition. All the company were now listening to the unbelievable blood-thirsty sports of the old days.

"My father told us of one of the best dogs belonged to Jem Wright, whose name was 'Kit', but there were many favourites. The bull would be baited all day and when he was tired the 'Berrod' would throw a bucket of water over him to refresh him. The best appreciated part was the 'smut'. This was when all the dogs were set on the bull at one time. Occasionally the bull was accidently let loose and then a general stampede finished up the day. Another amusement of the neighbourhood was cockfighting. The most celebrated cock pit was one kept by Joseph Lewis at Crabbs Cross.

Val told them that he had delighted them long enough with old stories. Val said they would join in the sing song. Bob had brought his mouth organ and Tom had a musical comb so with gusto their voices, young and old, became loud and clear as they chorused, 'Goodbye Dolly I must leave you,' 'Keep the home fires burning,' 'It's a long way to Tipperary' and 'Love is the sweetest thing'. Despite everything the year had thrown at them Val heard Edward say it was one of the best Christmases that they had ever had "Except Dad wasn't here" he said solemnly.

CHAPTER TWELVE

TALES RETOLD

James, in full swing, was unstoppable and as the young boys begged for more stories especially of Moses Shrimpton, Tom had heard it many times before, but still egged him on.

"Well" said James, making sure his glass was full, went on, "Moses Shrimpton was a notorious poacher and on a winter's night in February about thirty five years ago, attacked and killed a young policeman, James Davies. It was a ghastly sight. It was reported by a witness that the flesh of the throat was torn open from ear to ear and the windpipe was exposed. There was blood all over the hands of the poacher. Anyway he was hanged for the foul deed and a crowd of two thousand people raised a cheer. The grave of P.C. James Davies has the words written on the bottom of the stone: 'Leaving an example of faithful service in his native country.' People from the village of Alvechurch have maintained P.C. Davies's grave since his murder. Even today fresh flowers are put at the foot of his tomb."

"The mothers can't hear us, Uncle James, tell us about the fighting," pleaded Tom. James took a swig and related,

"My father told us of how sometimes the people in anticipation of a 'big mill' would collect a purse and persuade two men to fight for it, as was the case at Headless Cross, when Tom Cook and J. Millington fought. Among the principal fighting men were three brothers, Arch of Alcester Heath, K. Heath and Batten of Beoley. This Batten was employed as keeper under the Earl of Plymouth on account of his plucky character. He went on all right until one night he got too much of the old ale at the Hall, and set about the footman upon whom he left his mark in so many places that he had to leave his situation. But of all the boxers, Smith, who kept the Plough at Tanworth was considered king. He often came over to the Fox and Goose, got the 'pointers' together, treated them well and then induced them to fight him. He was a huge man with extraordinary strength of limbs, and it was frightful to see and hear him hit when he warmed into the fray.   One day he went to Hall Green races and was staring at Chappell's showmen.   The showman suggested that if Smith would keep his mouth open he (Chappell) would like the privilege of jumping down his throat.   Some 'chafing' went on and Smith offered to fight anyone of the troupe for twenty pounds and young Chappell was fixed upon to give him a good drubbing.   But he did not know his man, for although he was a wonderful fighter and gave Smith a good dressing down, he was obliged, at last, to strike his colours and bite the dust.

Smith had another great fight, beating Dunne, at Tanworth on the eleventh July about eighty five years ago. Fights used to take place chiefly in the Pound Meadow, on the green at Crabbs Cross, Mappleborough Green, and at the old White Hart, Headless Cross and later in the Bushy Piece.

The most terrible fighting I ever witnessed was at the White Hart, between a lot of 'pointers', who having met there to spend a quiet day, found the time hanging rather heavily on their hands, so, by way of variety turned out for a fight.

They paired themselves according to weight, and made the arrangement that no one should be permitted to fight more than three rounds, but these could be as long as they could make them.   Knowing therefore, how little time they had to do 'business in' you may imagine the manner in which they set to work and the execution they did.   Later, my father saw something of the same kind in Blind Lane, where, while one pair were having their turn, the surrounding friends were making arrangements to 'keep the pot boiling' and at the White Hart once during an affair of this kind, 'Nail' Styley was so anxious to fight anybody that, at last, Dick Stevens consented to his wishes, knocked him on top of a wood pile, and would not let him come down again until he promised to 'be good'.

At the time when the Birmingham to Worcester Canal was being cut at Tardebigge there was a good deal of fighting with the navvies, who were wont to come over in the evening and amuse themselves after their day's toil, with fighting the Redditch men in the Pound Meadow.   But the most Donnybrook-like affair you ever saw was once at Foxlydiate Wake, when about forty navvies came over to engage the chivalry of Redditch.   Everybody was obliged to fight or run.   There was no 'idle hands left to do mischief' of a certain party often spoken of by my father.   From fists they came to sticks - it was said that the navvies were provided with loaded ones.   Palings were pulled up, and a kid pile being handy, all armed themselves and turned into Mr. Hemming's meadow and fought until the navvies cut their sticks after having had serious if not fatal injuries inflicted on two of their 'Buddies'.

After that fighting became unfashionable and that which was once abundantly seen on every high hill, and under every green tree, became a rare occurrence. There followed other foolhardy entertainments shown especially to strangers to the town. When an unknown person passed in the locality the boys would 'heave half a brick at him' as a practical joke.

Shaving horses' tails, cutting harness were among some of the heartless and senseless of their 'larks'. Sometimes when a pedlar came to one of the needle mills, a party would engage his attention at one of the lower windows while another from above would pour a bucket of 'dotment' over the poor fellow and his cast iron knives, and, when he expressed his disapproval of the proceeding, they would drag him through the mill pond which would fix the grease rather than remove it.

Eventually the more vicious games were abandoned and their energies channelled in other directions which makes us what we are today, the smartest and quickest witted of men."

"Hoorah," said Jimmy.

"Well told," agreed Tom.

The ladies returned to the sitting room having returned the kitchen and living room back to normal.

CHAPTER THIRTEEN

THE BRAVE NEW WORLD

The splendour of Christmas was over and had greatly impoverished Val's larder, Post Office Savings and her health. The holiday had called for new clothes and boots for Edward and Tom and, as Topsy would be starting Bridge Street School soon that would mean a new outfit for her. It had all drained her purse miserably. There seemed to be a new spurt of enterprise in the town. Mr. Edwards had already taken on two new farm hands. The start of the promised Brave New World. It hadn't been a hard winter but Val felt a dull anti climax.

As she listened to the bells from St. Stephen's Church she recalled Mr. Edwards's words when she had lost Alf,

"Why is everything so hard, Val?" Val's pallor and unnatural irritability made Mary anxious so she insisted Val should see Dr. Burns this very morning. All the necessary chores had been taken care of and Val had made an appointment to see him at nine o'clock in Worcester Road. Val guessed his reaction.

"Put it down to your age, Mrs. Thomas. Here's a bottle of medicine to be taken three times a day before meals," his usual comment. This was a despair she hadn't felt for ages and sensibly came to the conclusion this was a down period in the rhythm of her life cycle. She told herself that it would pass. 'By the end of January I'll be back to routine' she thought, forever the optimist. Still the black thoughts persisted. What if this breathlessness was serious? What would happen to the children? Momentarily her self pity vanished as Mary, stirring the porridge sang softly to herself and Val shamefacedly counted her blessings.

"Get the boys off to school Mary. I'll take Topsy with me to Clarry's. Tell Mr. Sisom I had an appointment with Doctor Burns. I'll be back tomorrow".

"Have some breakfast first mam or you'll be feeling faint again like the other day at the factory."

"Yes. I'll take a bowl of bread and milk. Topsy can have her breakfast at Clarry's."

Later in the doctor's waiting room the uneasy silence was broken only by patients shifting their heads occasionally to study the next person coming through the door. Sitting in the corner a slightly built middle aged lady sat completely motionless. One would have mistaken her for a statue except for the piercing blackberry coloured eyes, (Clarry would have said like two burnt holes in a blanket) that darted every so often to the door with a nervous air of expectancy. Although the clothes she wore were spotless, it seemed as though they had been made for a much larger body. The sleeves well over the wrists and the epaulettes well over the narrow shoulders. Even the black serviceable shoes were laced tightly to encase the pointed, delicate feet, as though she had recently lost much weight.

At the end of the room sat a smartly dressed older gentleman. The aquiline nose and chin gave him an inbuilt alertness that his age had not wearied. His brown eyes glinted with the joy of living as though his mind had raked over all the fun he'd known for such dull moments as these.

Near to Val sat a young boy of about ten years deeply engrossed in a comic paper. His school cap was placed on his head at a jaunty angle, one red bordered sock was drawn neatly below his knee, but the other had collapsed to his ankle and as he swung his legs it seemed he was lost to the world. The hushed room was soon broken by the cries of a baby as a young mother struggled through the narrow doorway. She was hugging a tightly wrapped blanketed bundle while a noisy querulous child of about four years clung to her skirt. Once settled on the long couch he began plagueing his mother with endless questions. At first they were personal,

"Why is that man laughing? Why is that lady wearing that hat?" Several meaningless threats were levelled at him by his mother, then the questioning became more banal.

"When is a jar not a jar?"

"I don't know," came the impatient reply.

"When it's a door silly."

The poor girl glanced at the other serious patients, colouring slightly and obviously praying for deliverance. On that, the bell rang, it was Val's turn to meet the doctor. At her disturbed request he gave her a thorough examination. She breathed a deep sigh of relief as he told her without alarm that there existed a slight infection, due merely to the bitter winds and gave her a prescription for a bottle of linctus. So, after collecting the cure from Bowcotts on the

Parade, she hurried down Prospect Hill to tell Clarry the good news.

The first day of the new year. The first day of the rest of my life, thought Val. Once inside Clarry's living room there was a bear hug from her friend as she said,

"What a relief, Val. You looked so worried this morning."

"Yes. I was so depressed, but that's vanished. You only realize your wealth when in the waiting room you see someone worse off than yourself.

There was a serenely beautiful woman came in after me. I heard her say, quite calmly, that she had to lose her left foot. I overheard her say that gangrene had set in whilst she was on duty as an ambulance driver in France. They says 'don't moan because you have no shoes, lest you should meet someone who has no feet.' Can you imagine that happening to us Clarry? All these children to rear."

"That's true Val. It don't bear thinking about. Anyway take off your coat and let's have a cuppa. I've managed to beg some real sugar at last."

"How's the girls been, Clarry?" Val asked, but she saw they were both contentedly playing at 'shops'. Bridie precociously asked,

"What would you like today madam?" resisting the temptation to put the sweet meat in her own mouth said, "This would please your baby." Topsy said,

"Thank you Bridie," and split it in two and they each chewed on the tasty tit bit.

Val and Clarry laughed and Val told her,

"Topsy starts school in three week's time."

"That's good. Now we're getting on. Bridie and Topsy can go together. Life should be easier then Val."

"You never seem under any stress Clarry. The least thing and I get my knickers in a knot. You are so comfortable."

"Well, Val, it takes all sorts to make a world. It wouldn't do for us all to be alike. How dull."

"Boredom is a thing that will never trouble you Clarry. I'll take Bridie back with us if you want some time to yourself Clarry. Alright? What isn't done today will remain undone. Bob has promised to redecorate the sitting room, whitewash the walls and stain the beams. The room has to be stripped, but there is tomorrow untouched yet. Bridie can have dinner with us and we'll bring her back in time for tea." The girls were tucked cosily in the family pram and were soon jogging over the deep rutted lane back to Keepers Cottage.

CHAPTER FOURTEEN

YOUNG MR. SISOM

It was coming up to Topsy's birthday on January fifteenth, so Val had arranged for a party on the Sunday. Nothing grand. Some jelly, a sugar cake and small gifts, but Topsy was old enough to realize it was 'her' day.

Bob had redecorated the sitting room. It didn't seem to take him long. Men seem to make jobs look so easy. Val had hung the new Jacobean patterned curtains in a different fashion, with a pleated pelmet across the top of the window. The rich jewel colours gave a solid quality, making a traditional background for the dark furniture. The familiar home-made pegged rug had been replaced by a radiant golden coloured woollen carpet that Val had ordered from the factory club catalogue. The whole effect was of elegant charm, but to gain this, some of the warm domesticity had been sacrificed. By the same token Val tried to picture 'Clarry in a ball gown' and couldn't decide if this new fashioned room appealed to her or not, but realized that you had to move with the times.

Quite early on the Sunday afternoon, Joanne appeared at the door.

"Can I come in Val? My dad says you'll soon be fed up with me keep coming around, but I've told him that you said you didn't mind and I love being with your Mary, she's such fun."

Val told her it was Topsy's birthday and that Mary was getting her to try on the party dress.

"Janet, my sister, made it for her. It's a wild rose pink. Go on up, you can hear them talking," said Val.

As she passed through the living room, Val told her,

"After tea, we're going over to Tardebigge visiting the wounded soldiers. Do you want to come? They will undoubtedly enjoy the company of you young people."

"Yes. I'd love to Val. Perhaps I could buy some Woodbines for their kitty. I'll go now up to Ma Clements on the hill."

"We shall start tea soon so don't be too long Jo. You know Bob doesn't like to be kept waiting." With a roguish chuckle Joanne answered,

"Don't worry about Bob. He'll wait for me. I just met him in the lane, he said that he'd wait for me anytime."

"Oh, did he?" said Val smiling, "He didn't tell me he'd seen you. I expect he forgot. You look ravishing in that coat, Jo. You should always wear that light green, it matches your eyes."

"Now, Val. You know in your heart I'm not half so pretty as your Mary, and nowhere near as kind or tender-hearted. Do you remember how she carried that wild kitten home in her handbag last week. She was nearly in tears. Did the poor little thing survive?"

"No" said Val, "We kept him in a shoe box for a week, but nevertheless its life throbbed away. Probably pined for its mother. But Mary tried hard to save him. Nursed him through all that first night. Our Mary would make a fine nurse."

"Yes. That's it, Val. Why don't you get her trained for the new nursing corps. That gentle touch and caring nature is needed badly in the Smallwood Hospital."

"You go now Jo or we'll never get tea over," Val urged. Joanne, she was as slender as a willow tree and, as Val watched the silk clad legs trip fleetingly across the yard could understand why all the factory lads spoiled her. Also, by the same common sense, knew there was more than sawdust beneath those raven black curls. Vera, who worked on the next bench to Val in the packing department crocheted woollen hats, usually in two contrasting shades. Val treated herself to a mauve and grey one and one for Mary in electric blue and shell pink. Joanne wore one of the same pattern today, white and mint green. It framed her doll-like face.

"You look like a spray of cherry blossom," Val had told her.

"Thanks for the compliment, Val," she had smiled. Full of youthful vitality, already aware of the spell she cast. Val had heard Ron, the new tool fitter say,

"I wish she'd say 'yes' to me." He said to Val that he would willingly give his high teeth for a meeting with the high spirited lass, but was scared of being branded 'a baby snatcher.'

Actually, she was older than the tripping neat footwork suggested. When she returned, Val asked her if she would enjoy a trip to the Lickey Hills with all the family at Easter. Joanne readily accepted.

CHAPTER FIFTEEN

A DAY ON THE LICKEY HILLS

Although Easter Monday dawned wild and chilly, Val had heard on the radio that the holiday would become much brighter by late afternoon.

Joanne came over about mid morning and Bob loaded up the trap with the basket that Val had well filled for lunch. Val had suggested Joanne should sit up front so that Val could control Edward and Tom behind. Topsy was thilled to pieces at the prospect of an exciting ride miles and miles away. They found a secluded spot near the pine woods with a fabulous view over Birmingham's city buildings. The boys were soon off along with the puppies to explore beyond the high fern fronds. Bob made a fire with the help of Mary and Joanne, while Val produced food like a magician producing rabbits from a hat.

At first Topsy was afraid to venture farther than the immediate picnic circle, but she did eventually step into the woods already misted blue by the bluebells. She came back triumphantly displaying her bouquet. The chubby grubby fists were full of the wild flowers.

Edward and Tom came rushing back after about an hour crying of hunger. Paste sandwiches, cornish pasties, cake, jelly, apple pie and tea and squash disappeared before you could say Jack Robinson.

"I want la pomme" Edward shouted.

"Take him over the hill behind the bilberry bushes Tom. He will be unseen down in that dell." Bob showed them the pathway. Val and Topsy had a snooze in the fitful sunshine. Bob played 'Jackie Five Stones' on the open patch with Joanne. Mary curled up with a magazine. Tom and Edward showed their skill at 'Tip Cat' while the puppies were kept lively by constantly retrieving the stick thrown periodically by Edward. As soon as the sun lost its warmth, for it was quite early in the year, they loaded back into the trap and Bob steered the pony down the country lanes through Barnt Green and finally when in Brockhill Lane they could

81

almost see home.

Joanne had again placed herself alongside Bob after Val had agreed. At Joanne's query Val had told her,

"Of course, dear. You can chat as you go along, but don't divert his attention too much."

The boys were exhausted and so were the dogs on their laps. Topsy had fallen asleep and was only prevented from falling by Tom's frantic grabs. Mary and her mother were squashed together, their feet resting on the picnic basket.

"That Joanne's a bit pushy don't you think mam?" Mary whispered.

"I could have sat by Bob going home. Didn't even ask me."

"Ssh Mary. She will think you're being jealous," her mother remonstrated.

"I wish I could like her better. Pure wantonness."

Val leaned forwards to ease a cramped leg and attempted to check the girl's chagrin.

"She doesn't go out very often," and almost inaudibly said,

"Selfish people need all the kindness in the world. We've tried to share our happiness with her and I'm sure she appreciates the gesture." The words sounded trite but they made a curious echo in her mind and in her loving heart.

Changing the drift of the conversation Val asked Mary,

"What are you wearing tomorrow. It's stock taking, so I should put on your long skirt. You will be climbing up and down those steps. Better not give the lads too much of an eyeful."

"Righto mother. I'll rinse out this blouse. It will be dry by morning." Bob urged the pony forward along the last empty stretch of road. At last in the home garden Val shouted,

"Come on lads. Can you carry Topsy, Tom? Get up Edward, we're home." In a deep sleep the baby struggled, threw out her arms and hurt herself. Val exchanged burdens, gave Tom the picnic basket now much lighter and took from him the crying child. Safe in Val's arms the crying ceased as there were comforting kisses placed on the bruised fingers.

"Not my fault," Tom exclaimed.

"I know Tom. It was an accident. I'll bathe it in cold water. It will soon be better. There, there baby. You'll be alright." Val consoled. When they were all indoors Val shouted to Joanne,

"You musn't be late home Jo. Your mother will worry after you."

"I'll go home about seven if that's alright with you Val.

I've had a smashing day with you all. Can I come again?"
"We'll see," came back Val's non-committal answer.
"Say 'yes' Val," she coaxed. "Let's go Whitsun Day.
I'll bring some strawberries and cream and a chocolate cake.
I know what Bob likes now."

Bob had ushered the lads into the yard, he rapped out
the instructions,

"Lock up the hens Tom, and you, Edward, can help me
get some spuds in." The voices died away. Mary was
getting Topsy ready for bed.

"She's so tired mam. Too tired to have her supper. I'll
give her a drink and take her upstairs."

"Thanks, Mary. That will be a help. I'll put the lads
clothes out for morning." Joanne came in from the scullery
where she had unpacked the remains of the picnic.

"It won't take me long Val to cross the market place
and down Unicorn Hill. I'll see about going when I've said
goodnight to Mary."

"Oh, you musn't walk all that way after such a tiring
day. Bob will give you a lift back."

"Here they are," she said as noises sounded at the door.

"Will you run Joanne home, Bob? Her mother would
never forgive me if I allowed her to walk home alone after
such a hectic day."

"Of course," and to Joanne, "You must be fagged out.
We'll go as soon as Sam's had a drink. We've had such a
topping day. Get your coat on I'll be back directly."

After taking Joanne home, Bob came back about nine
and appeared strangely quiet. Val believed he would be too
fatigued to bring in the morning sticks and coal for the early
fire as usual, but although he did this ungrudgingly he soon
left, not even waiting for his cheese and cocoa.

The following Thursday Val was searching for Joanne
down on the shop floor. She had left her gloves in the
cottage under the sideboard. Val had found them while
chasing Topsy's woollen ball. They must have fallen behind
the dresser last weekend. As Val passed at the end of the
factory door leading to the machine shop Phil's voice could
be heard:

"Well, does you know, kid? I went to the pictures and
you sees this young girl stretched across the railway lines.
Just as it gets exciting up comes the caption 'to be continued
next week'. So I'll have to wait until next Saturday to see
what happens to Pearl White." On seeing Val the flow of
words quietened and Phil asked if she was better.

"Yes thanks Phil," Val told her. "Joanne's been telling
us what a lovely time you all had on Easter Monday," Phil

said. Joanne came over and putting an arm around Val's waist went through all the things they had enjoyed at Lickey Hills.

"Yes, Val's promised to take me again. Haven't you Val?" glancing hopefully at Val playing for confirmation, but again Val wouldn't be drawn and again told the girl,

"We'll see."

"Mary likes your company. She hasn't stopped talking about your new button up shoes and smart velvet dress. She even copies the way you trip around, and your lisp as you sound your 's's'. You know what a mimic she is. She's not allowed to wear make up yet.

"Does your mother object to your scarlet lipstick?"

"She doesn't see it. Make sure it's off before I get home. My mother's a fuddy duddy. Not like you Val, generous and lighthearted."

"I'm sure she adores you. Don't grow up too quick Joanne. As Phil will tell you, the best things in life are worth waiting for." Val tried to stem the impossible enthusiasm of youth.

"That's my trouble Val. I just can't wait."

"Anyway Jo. Come to us anytime. You're so lively. We're nearly always at home and Bob said he will walk you home. He's a good lad."

CHAPTER SIXTEEN

BOB'S WEAKNESS

The hawthorn was already quickening with a haze of green foliage this spring day, and although Bob had dug over the patch for the planting of new vegetables at the cottage, Val had felt an alien aloofness in his manner. The old undivided attentiveness became variable. The withdrawn manner and fatuous laughter made him a stranger and Val wondered if some illness had struck him.

His regular tender questioning of her needs were gone and even last night she had mentioned that there were no sticks or coals prepared, he had flatly answered that other things were more important.

She realized her need of his support was greater now than previously, for the official letter, still in her hand, contained alarming news. It had stated that as Mr. Edwards needed to employ a farm manager to deal with the post war methods of farming it meant he needed Val's cottage to rehouse the extra staff.

"It is with regret Mrs. Thomas that I require you to vacate Keepers Cottage a month from today." She had one month to find another home. That would not be easy with four children. She thought 'Bob will be here tonight, I will tell him "Yes" even for the children's sake. She would give him the answer he had been pressing for. It was May, a superb time to be married. Later on in the day while at work Val had made her usual tour of the machine shop giving out the work rotas, and over the clatter of the shuffling blades of the cleaning machine, Val heard Winnie say,

"No, her's not here. Didn't yer know? Her's preggers. The father? I doon't know. Nobody knows. Her never goes out much. Her woon't even tell her mam. I knows. I knows. You needn't tell me 'her shouldn't 'a dropped 'em." There were muffled sniggers and the gossip like the machines went on and on.

At dinner time Val made a special visit downstairs and

asked Winnie where Joanne was.   Winnie bent down suddenly to pick up a loose swivel from amongst the shale on the shop floor, as an excuse to avoid Val's innocent questioning.

"Nellie's just told me 'ers sick.   The 'flu.   There's a lot abate in the lane."   Winnie gave out a statement, it seemed she expected to be contradicted, and, through lack of confidence, was terrified of uttering controversial hearsay, lest she should become involved.   Val herself, until latter years, had experienced this diffidence, so sympathised with the timid woman's gossip and told her,

"I'll pay her a visit before I go home.   She hasn't explained the reason why she didn't turn up last Sunday at our house for tea.   Mary nor me have heard a word from her for over a week."   Val asked Mary to slip in and tell Clarry that she would be late home.

After work, it didn't take Val long to cross the town, down Unicorn Hill and along Bromsgrove Road.   Once inside the porch at Joanne's house, Val fingered the fruit she had bought from Tom Smith's, wondering if Joanne cared for blood oranges.

Mr. Broden opened the door and passed on the information that Joanne and her mother had left about an hour ago on a trip to the doctor's in Worcester Road.   "They're taking a short cut up Littleworth so they shouldn't be long.   Perhaps you would like to wait in the sitting room, Mrs. Thomas.   I'll make you a cup of tea," he kindly suggested.

"Thanks," Val replied, "I might as well wait, now I'm here.   Mary and Joanne get on like a house on fire.   She's older than my Mary and I think Mary's a mite jealous.   She's promised to come to Bidford on Sunday.   I hope she will be better by then.   I'd heard she'd caught the 'flu infection so I've brought her some fruit.   I will wait a short while if you don't mind.   When is she coming back to work?"   Val asked concernedly.

"I'm not sure.   See her mother when they come back. You've been very good to Joanne.   Settling her in her new job, and she loves coming to your house.   Her mother and me left it late in life to have a baby so she thinks we're old fashioned.   She loves the youth and vitality of your loving home Mrs. Thomas.   I hope she hasn't imposed on your kindness too much."

"Not at all," Val called after him as he murmured again,

"The tea, it won't be five minutes."   Joanne's father disappeared through the hall into the rear kitchen from where there came a welcome clatter of tea cups.

Val's memory recalled the fact Joanne's parents were

ambitious that she should become a musician and envied the superb quality of the piano set against the far wall. Probably the young girl had found it tiresome that her parents' insistence that there must be regular practise. Joanne had tried to explain the skills of Miss Griffin but said she still found the practise boring. Val could never imagine Joanne as a dedicated student for she wanted results too quickly. Everything had to be now, for Joanne's impulsive nature, but it would be interesting to see the choice of music available nowadays.

Val opened the stool top to check the scores. She found a copy of usual exercise, 'Cradle song', 'Poor 'ol Joe' and a few of the more modern pieces, 'Skylark' and 'Don't go down the mine, daddy'. The pages were shifted as Val tried to hum the tunes. From the centre of the pile a white card dropped to the floor.

"Oh, goodness" sighed Val, "I've disturbed her 'exam' paper. This must be the result from the college."

She bent hurriedly to retrieve the fallen missive from the shiny, oil-cloth-covered floor. With a guilty tidying of the many sheets she said under her breath shamefacedly I'd better return all this sheet music before Mr. B. comes back.

The back of the card was pristine white and then she turned it face upwards. But, wonderingly saw it wasn't an examination report. It was a recently taken photo of Bob. Her Bob. What was that doing here? I've never given a photo of Bob to anyone. Least of all to Joanne, she thought. Val actually had witnessed a display of the callousness of youth not long since when Joanne had given a demonstration of the poor chap's limping manner. Val thought at the time what a cheap joke, but put it down to the immaturity of Joanne's mind.

The surprise turned to a deeper despair when, almost subconsciously she read the bold printing beneath the picture, 'To my beloved Jo from Bob. xxxx' She returned the photo to its hiding place as though it was searing hot. As she fled from the house she struck viciously at the Virginia creeper that had momentarily barred her way, as it had grown across the doorway.

In truth there was no need to confront Bob on the issue because now all the minute details came flooding back to torment her. "He'd had to fetch Jo's shoes from Mr. Hawthorn's". "Jo wanted him to repair her bike". "I'll take Jo and the boys to Boscoe's". "I haven't time to stop for supper." She recalled when asked, if the daily chores of getting in the coals had been done he'd answered indifferently,

"Can't Edward do it for you, Val?" When, eventually

87

Val reached Clarry's house, the flame of indignation showed in a new nervousness, as the old sense of hysteria threatened and Val's breathing became laboured.

No need for explanation to Clarry. Immediately Val showed her face, Clarry sensed some stress had caused her friend's obvious disturbance.

"Well," said Clarry, after hearing the details, "Men are such fools. Give em an inch and they'll take a yard. Like James' old mother often told me,

"The only time you know where your man or your dog is, is the time you have them by the scruff of the neck," and Clarry grabbed a cushion to demonstrate.

"I suppose that's perfectly true, Clarry. I never dreamed, not for one moment. How could this have gone on so long without him having the courage to tell me?"

"Perhaps he didn't want to hurt you Val. But it seems everyone else knew. Winnie was in Webb's. I thought she was kidding when she told me. But they say the wife is always the last one to know. If it's a case, he'll have to marry her," Clarry went on shooing Michael into the other room. "None of your business" she shouted to him and to Val she said,

"Serves Bob right. It will break his mother's heart if it's true. There's never smoke without fire. Will you see him again?"

"No. There's no use in stretching the pain further. What's done cannot be undone. But it would have to happen now. I've heard today Mr. Edwards wants the cottage for the new farm manager. I shall miss you desperately Clarry. I'll have no one."

"Now then Val. This is not like you. As one door shuts another opens. Take heart. But I must tell you this. I've watched him taking young Joanne home these long warm summer evenings and I've mentioned it to James. You know what that girl is for flashing her thighs. They see the power they hold over a man and it unhinges their morals. I daren't voice my fears to you, love, for fear I was mistaken. But there's no mistaking that look on a healthy man's face, even a cripple, when thrown together with a girl for any length of time."

"Yes, I suppose I took his love for granted. He loved me truly, but I kept him dangling too long, but that's all over now. I'm all alone again. All this worry of moving house. Do you know of a small place to let Clarry? This is a dreadful time. You can't imagine the weakness to feel so vulnerable," Val sighed.

"Yes Val. Now you realized you're a widow. But the

boys are growing up. Mary is an angel and your Topsy is so adorable, she'll soon be off your hands at Bridge Street.

"They're all I've got now. The children and plenty of work and worry. Pray to give me strength to rear them Clarry. I shouldn't feel too bad. I've still got your friendship. I don't know how I'd have managed without you. You've been kindness itself to me."

'Ha, away wi ye. That's what friends are for, come over later and we'll drown our sorrows in a cuppa."

"Thanks love, I will, " Val promised.

Bob never showed his face again, and the boys uncannily enough never said they missed him. Perhaps with the gossip heard in the playground repeated by parents they had come to terms with the situation in a brave way. Mary could not forgive Bob for his treachery and made herself particularly loving and tender to her mother. She wouldn't hear his name mentioned.

"He's gone children. Good riddance to bad rubbish. We shall manage without him," Mary told them in brave defiance.

It meant more tasks for each and everyone of them but they shouldered this uncomplainingly. They were a family and pulled together as their father had taught them. Val said,

"Let's only remember the good things Bob did for us and be grateful for that. It's all part of life's rich pattern", Val consoled as her optimism looked set to endure.

To my beloved Jo
from Bob
xxxx

CHAPTER SEVENTEEN

IT NEVER RAINS

Val had heard through Phil, of all people, of a small house to rent. In this case her endless gossip had proved positive and so Val had moved into the end house of a row of six in Edward Street. It was two and six per week for rental, but even that seemed to come too regular for Val's liking for, although she did earn better money now in the packing department due to keen punctuality and attention to detail. She was now put in charge but the bills fell like leaves in autumn. Mary was still shaping swivels for fishing lines in the machine shop, but George had promised to find her a place in the packing department as soon as the opportunity arose.

The house move had used Val's savings, as it was absolutely necessary to buy new linoleum for the downstairs. It was not possible to cover the upstairs floors at the same time so there were still bare boards in the bedrooms, but Val hoped to remedy this before winter. This house was a much better location. Nearer the shops, school and station. But with four children to clothe and feed the opening of a pawn shop on Unicorn Hill proved a source of income when Val became desperate. Granny Ross was a keen business lady, but the hard luck stories became an everyday occurrence. Many heart breaking stories were told. One man pawned his false teeth to buy some meat, then, without his teeth, he couldn't eat it. The town was not without its share of sad war widows and many children went barefoot.

It was coming up to Mary's birthday. Val had bargained for an old blouse at Granny Ross's to give Mary as a present. It didn't look very special when Val had sorted it out from the bundle on the counter, but, when Val soaked it overnight in Hudson's powder it came up a deep apricot colour. It had a dainty stand-up lace collar, and tiny pearl buttons richly decorating the front bodice, and after Val's clever fingers added bows of velvet to the cuffs and collar then rinsed it in a thin starch, ironing it when quite damp with the flatiron, the finished garment looked superb. It could have come straight from the catwalks of Paris fashion for only sixpence, and a great deal of effort and imagination.

Harry was invited to the tea-party. He said his father would bring him round about seven. Clarry had produced a decorated cake. The children had spread out to the tiny garden until tea was ready. Mr. Hendley brought Harry early, so Val took the opportunity of inviting him into the sitting room. He was reluctant at first, but later agreed to look over the home.

"You've made it comfy, Mrs. Thomas. You've been so kind to my son since we moved here."

"He's so well-behaved. We love having him. So artistic. You should see the tower he and Tom built from matchsticks. Such patience and dexterity. We miss the animals, but Mr. Edwards insisted the boys go to the farm whenever they have time. He was very practical and agreed to move most of the heavy things on the farm cart. And, of course, the assistance of you and your van was greatly appreciated. Will you stay to tea Mr. Hendley?"

"No, thanks. I won't stay. I'll pick Harry up later? Tell me if he misbehaves," he begged.

Val would have enjoyed his company but still that aloof wall pervaded and he left the house with a brief handshake.

"Bye, bye, Mrs. Thomas, and thanks again." There was a gentle sincerity in the serious, brown eyes.

"Please call me Valerie" she invited. She almost came to questioning his cool approach but modesty forbade it and instead told him,

"I'll see he's ready in time Mr. Hendley," and there was no Christian name familiarity in her reply. After the party, true to his word he came to collect the boy, it was very quiet, all the others had gone earlier.

Val's boys and Harry were playing 'hide and seek' in the yard, Mary had accompanied Clarry and Bridie to half way house. Topsy was in bed.

"Come along young man," Mr. Hendley called to his son, "Mrs. Thomas might as well adopt you. You're here more often than you are at home."

"I would willingly adopt him. It's an experience to see his delicate and refined movements. And he will be corrected which is a good trait for a young person. To see a flaw and set about altering it immediately. If I told my Tom he'd made a mistake he would sulk for days.

"His grandfather was a craftsman. He sat for hours completing the trellis work on a card table for my mother. Although weary there would be examination and re-examin-

91

ation until he was completely satisfied every detail was perfect. My mother found such accuracy tiresome, but all was forgiven when she possessed an article of beauty to last forever. I still have the table. It is a rarity. You must come to see it one day. I'll leave it to you in my will", he laughed.

"I would feel privileged, but please don't talk of wills. You have an exciting life before you. You have freedom and ability. The world is your oyster." But Val felt a weary futility as though she were talking to a blind and deaf person. At a thought that she had crossed the bounds of politeness she said,

"I'll fetch Harry's coat."

Such was the man's vibrant personality that the mere fact of passing close to him caused her heart to beat wildly. At a distance this magnetism could be ignored, but here, face to face with her idol, it was impossible to avoid that over-powering quality of the man's tranquility and confident bearing. Val knew it would have been heavenly to lay against the support of that strong shoulder and unburden her heart. In dreams she had accepted a meaningful kiss from those strong and sensitive lips. The thought remained there, in a divine dream only.

He didn't appear annoyed at her observations, merely painfully aloof, but his friendly humorous tone brought her back to earth.

"What have you got there. Pandora's Box?" Val smiled for she had returned with Harry's coat also a box of cakes left over from the party.

"Yes, you can open it and prove if the adage is true that 'Hope springs eternal in the human breast'." She sounded too flippant to be at ease, although she savoured every second of that exquisite encounter.

She noticed the fine, black hairs showing beneath the cuffs of his cream coloured shirt as he put on the boy's over-coat. He relieved her of the box with thanks and as an after-thought chided with a roguish grin,

"Don't be too inquisitive. Remember the legend." This warm and intimate dialogue only made the situation even more mysterious. She felt such sweet emotion of half-pity, half-desire. His eyes were too vital with delight to register any particular colour, but she glimpsed flecks of azure flash as he continued to tease. Val felt frail and futile before his penetrating gaze. Commonsense forbade her to bring forth any direct questions and she puckered her brow in a quizzical study, willing him fervently to enlighten her on his life's ambitions, but soon found a spiritual fatigue

in attempting to unfathom the unfathomable. He bade
Harry to thank Mrs. Thomas and say 'Goodnight' while
effortlessly he reached for the door handle and was gone.

Even this casual conversation gave Val a happy stream
of emotion although there still existed an unreality of normal
life that her instinct told her these gossamer threads of
friendship were rare. The man remained an enigma.

As she watched them disappearing into the distance she
remembered the bleak words,

"When hope has kindled hope and lured thee to its
brink." Her thoughts were stunted and frustrated so she
soon busied herself with the 'common round, the daily task'
of preparing the children's clothes for school. That had been
three months ago. There had been no sign of Mr. Hendley
either in the town or at the factory when the perceptive Phil
ventured,

"I haven't seen your hero for a long time Val." Val
coloured slightly, for his world, and the busy industrious
factory world, seemed so far apart.

"No," was all Val could utter, as though, even the
mention of him seemed too sacred to involve in common
gossip.

Phil never gave in easily and pressed on,

"Are you in love with him, Val? You are an incurable
romantic," and with the tactless direct way of all gossips she
gave a direct stare at Val and asked,

"Has he ever asked you out?"

"No," said Val, offering no explanation for there was
none.

"Perhaps he's still in love with his wife." With almost
instant defence Val declared quickly,

"He is a mystery. But he is a genuine person, his
sincerity is real. I'm positive he's no philanderer. I haven't
seen him for ages." She made a careful calculation, "must
be three months or more. It was our Mary's birthday."

"He's so handsome," Phil said, trying to give genuine
comfort. "Perhaps he's playing hard to get."

"No" said Val, "that's not his style. They say indifference is worse than hate. If only there was some explanation
for his sadness. Oh, well, it takes all sorts, Phil," and
changing the subject asked,

"How's our Mary getting on with you all?"

"Very well. She's shy, but then she's young. But we'll
soon knock the corners off her. Only yesterday Simon, the
new lad on maintenance shouted at her,

"Your lace petticoat is showing Mary."

"Defiantly your Mary shouted back,"

"Well, it's clean and paid for, washed and cared for, if you don't like it, what do you stare for?" Yes, she's getting to be one of us Val." Val moved back upstairs not relishing the thought of her gentle darling 'having the corners knocked off her' as Phil suggested.

Today was an early October day, there was a fitful sun, but it gave no real warmth, still it brightened up the copper beaches in St. Stephen's churchyard. Val loved these dry crisp days so she decided to walk up to Crumpfields to visit Janet who had proudly presented a son to the world.

She decided to walk through Foxlydiate Lane and coming to the stream at the foot of Springhill paused for a moment to watch the traffic on the swollen waters. She leaned over the rustic bridge wishing for the company of Mr. Hendley. Phil was right. He was handsome, and intelligent and caring. 'Strange' she mused, 'he's a complete stranger yet I love the very bones of the man. Why does he haunt me so?' Val thought 'One can bear sadness alone, sadness was invented for lonely people. It's only when beauty and joy are available that one needs company. Beauty is made for sharing.'

The autumn rains had gathered much flotsam and jetsam on the flowing water beneath the country style bridge and the creamy foam at the water's edge seemed to frame the whole moving picture. She watched amused as scattering the fallen leaves a bush tailed squirrel in his russet coloured coat was burrowing for his winter stores.

It was truly fascinating to watch the twigs and leaves surging on the brook's surface, each item in movement. Some forming groups, some clinging to a like-piece and shifting with the water's waves as a pair, while others sailed on making their own way alone. The seething, searching crowds were each intent on finding their own level, and the problems displayed, seemed to match the unanswered quest in her own heart.

Eventually she bade farewell to the water's hidden message leaving the stream to carry its burden on to the rushing, pounding climax of the main river.

Before she left the lane she looked back at the tiny hamlet and the cottage where poor Mrs. Middleton had met her untimely end. It was a particularly gruesome murder back in 1902. A hard-working mother was killed by her drunken husband in a row over money. The husband had killed his wife and set fire to the house. The report stated that 'the crime was more shocking than one would have expected to see in the lowest slums of Liverpool or other thickly populated places where crime is more or less epidemic.' Val thought of the poor woman's last moments and shuddered after all these years she was glad to hurry on to Webheath, and a more cheerful errand. She made her way down the long drive that led to Janet's home, Lindenwood, marvelling that the fuchsia's ruby drops still looked rich and vibrant, and there were still scarlet and gold dahlias spangling the border.

By the time she reached her sister's bedroom the harsher part of her chagrin had eased, and all feeling of her desolation vanished at the sight of her nephew. He was such a minute bundle.

Janet invited her to hold him and, as Val breathed in deeply at the open crevice at the baby's neck, and caressed the cocooned armful of bliss, silly words tumbled from her lips as she expressed the joy of holding the precious fragment so near, so dear to her.

"What a cherub Jan. He's scrumptious. Such a darling," Val exclaimed ecstatically. She handed the tiny form back to his mother and enquired,

"What are going to call him?"

"What do you suggest?" Janet asked. It was obvious Janet loved the tender, caring nature of her elder sister and was pleased to involve her in her own happiness, for Val had looked so care worn of late, as though 'a worm in the bud fed on her damask cheek' as Shakespeare wrote long ago.

"See what's fashionable Val. There's the Indicator." Janet pointed to the folded paper at her bedside table. Val eagerly obliged, saying as she unfolded each page,

"There's been a spate of Fredericks and Pauls. Her voice faded to a whisper as, looking down the column of Births, Deaths and In Memory notices a name stood out in white fire - Oliver Hendley died September 30th. Her sight blurred as the black and white letters spelt their sad message. Facts are stubborn things. But there it was, stark and final. No more mystery. Looking at the innocent sleeping baby at his mother's side Val enquired softly,

"Will you call him Oliver?"

Janet mused on this and divining her sister's genuine desire said thoughtfully,

"Yes. That's a strong name, we'll call him Oliver." Val moved to the window that gave a rural picture over Lower Bentley. She saw the compact setting of the distant village snuggled in the hollow, surrounded by tall poplars and ancient oaks. It expressed safety and security as the blue-grey smoke spiralled from the cluster of cottages towards the sky. As her eyes traced the pattern which usually foretold a fine day to come, she observed how the pearly beads of cloud had rolled away showing a glimpse of the heavenly blue beyond and, even as she watched, the white fringes closed gently together. Her lips tingled as she tasted the kiss of an angel, hearing again the haunting melody, 'For love is ended before it began.'

"I'll care for your boy. Goodnight, God bless, Oliver."

CHAPTER EIGHTEEN

LIFE IN THE YARD

The injustices of misery and poverty had aged Val and the reflection she saw in the mirror seemed a total stranger. Although her neighbours were kindness personified Val couldn't get used to sharing washing and toilet facilities in the yard. As long as she remained "one of them" there was harmony, but Val experienced from their usual gossip that if one should make a moral lapse or acquire a new home addition which proved beyond their reach, then the smiles and bows turned to jealousy, and the criticism was severe and hurtful. The spectre of near starving people was not pleasant. The compassion of the ministers who had promised a new world fit for heroes to live in was inadequate and never materialised.

Val's neighbours, indeed she knew, most of the hard working souls in that yard existed from one meagre pay day until the next, sometimes not knowing where the next meal was coming from.

A few beef bones and vegetables from the allotment was a daily menu. The local store, too, must have suffered, for in the week, most shopping was obtained 'on the strap' and the familiar chant 'I'll pay the end of the week' was heard. Some of the less trusted customers paid on Friday, but by the following Monday they were 'on the strap' again. The diet was pitiable and Val's Topsy developed ricketts and Val was advised to bathe her legs in potato water, which proved successful.

Mary had at last been given the job of clerical work in the packing department at Milwards and Val was not unmindful of the sneers and snide remarks. Phil said,

"When I told Winnie her was being moved to the packin' her looked at me 'gone' ate. Her's jealous. Take a lot of no notice Val."

Although unemployment was rife for men in the heavier industries, Redditch provided plenty of the finer, more delicate work of fly dressers, finishing of needles and knitting

97

pins for the women folk; the small factories producing needles of every size and need, but conditions were poor, and, the effects of needle pointing were shown in the following lines by E. Elliot:

> There draws the grinder his laborious breath,
> There coughing at his deadly trade he bends,
> Born to die young, he fears no man, nor death,
> Scorning the future, what he earns he spends,
> Yet Abraham and Elliot both in vain
> Bid science on his cheek prolong the bloom,
> He would not live! he seems in haste to gain
> The undisturbed asylum of the tomb,
> And, old at two and thirty, meets his doom.

Eventually fans were introduced to extract the pollution from the work shop, and the factory owners were obliged to provide milk daily for these particular workers on needle pointing. The humility of the terraced houses and communal courts were grim, although the conditions could not stifle the vitality and basic desire to better oneself. The few progressive workers urged the new labour government to better education for their children and better housing. Unfortunately the labour representatives could not compare with the wealthy, for the working class stalwarts were largely inarticulate, and themselves uneducated, but gradually this was remedied. It entailed a moral and a class judgment. But the women folk were mostly in perpetual motion, trying to rear a family and tackle some jobs in the nearby factory in an effort to keep the wolf from the door, so that despite the brave and valuable winning of the suffragette's battle to enable women to vote, not many used it to advantage. They were either too ignorant of the votes' effect or too busy. The men had their pint of beer and packet of Woodbines and the more industrious an allotment to work on at weekends.

Val struggled on each day, mostly going from bed to work, hoping one day to have her own privacy in a separate house with separate toilet facilities. It seemed such a distant dream.

There were days of gloom and depression lightened only by someone's unquenchable humour when one could see the 'funny side'. Bill Teague said that the 'wolf wasn't only at the door, but that he'd come inside and had pups.' Another mother plagued with the inevitable question,

"What's for dinner?"

"Duck"

"Duck?"

"Yes, duck under the table." Val heard Mrs. Thomas's lad, Sam, say,

"This bread's dry mam." The poor distraught woman answered,

"Well, take it to the pump and wet it."

Life was one continual fight against poverty and disease, and, the weak fell by the wayside. They either took to the 'bottle' or the 'streets'.

Freda Simkins was often seen in Birmingham Road complete with white handbag, it seemed this was a badge of the 'oldest profession' known. But Bill Clements from Britain Street said humorously that times were so bad that she was a virgin.

Val was a survivor and inspired the immediate neighbours to a better standard. In the meantime she pulled her weight and in turn kept the communal areas well scrubbed, and neat parcels of newspaper strung behind the door on a nail in the outside lavatory. The seats were well scoured with Jey's fluid, the walls and ceilings whitewashed and drains scalded with boiling soda water to kill the germs. Emmie Long's door step was whitened every morning before she crossed the road to Abel Morrell's factory. There were sluts who lost the fight and sank lower and lower in degradation. One, Brummie Maggie they called her, made her evening jaunts down Birminham Road complete with her badge.

She told Emmie that she had a pen friend, and that one day this pen friend turned up on Maggie's doorstep.

"I dain't know 'e was cumin. Any road up' e took one look at me in me curlers, an' cup 'o gin in me 'and, an I never seen or 'eard from 'im since."

"I wonder why," said Emmie sarcastically. For the most part, in that yard where Val lived, they were diligent and respectable. The family unit the main concern. With the demands of raising a family, sewing, mending, cooking, also an outside job there was not much time for social life. Their main communication, meeting in the brewhouse or trooping to and fro to the outside lavatory.

Val had one loyal friend Emmie Workman, who had long surrendered to the blight of middle age, but she was a homely, domesticated body who was trusted and welcomed in Val's home. Although she never told Val herself, it was said that she existed on a crust of bread most days so that the children were satisfied, but she was too proud to ask or accept a mouthful from any of her neighbours.

It was a close community, more from necessity than choice. Each knew what time each particular neighbour rose from his bed, exact time he went out in the morning, the colour coat they would wear that day. How many times they went to the toilet, and why. The young females were regarded religiously lest they should stray from the straight and narrow path. It was not always an harmonious one, especially Friday nights when the men came home from The Fox, shouting obsceneties, baiting a fellow neighbour to settle some score. Dibby Cook was ready to challenge the whole row on a Friday night. Next morning he would be up bright as a button ready for work remembering nothing of the night before.

There were many quaint nicknames. Because Lindy Cook rejected their advances, whether honourable or otherwise, they called her 'little Miss Pissquick'. Frousty Freda and Fanny Fewtrell plied their miserable trade. Emmie was the only one encouraged to come into Val's house. They would work on a rug or a bit of knitting, sometimes they would share a parcel of homework from Morrells, putting heads on safety pins.

Val read her prayer book everyday and realised God didn't allow his children to stay on the peaks of suffering for long. Her days continued to be occupied fully, but she longed to have her own washhouse and toilet on her own.

It was pitiable when the rent man called to witness the embarrassment of certain tenants who had indulged in extras and overspent the meagre budget. Emmie used to say to Val,

"There's only two things you can be sure of in this world, that's death and the rent man."

It seemed it was Maggie's greatest ambition to avoid or delay the rent man at all costs. Emmie told Val that, one day Maggie lay flat on the floor pretending she was not there, but the persistent fellow opened the letter box and they stared at each other eye to eye. Emmie said she had to let him in, and he got his rent. She didn't say how.

It was a dreary, soul destroying existence and Val prayed fervently for deliverance, vowing to Emmie that should the opportunity ever occur in the future, it would be her first endeavour to ease the burden of these poor hapless women.

Some days at the 'low cycle' or the monthly 'curse', she knew despair, but with a natural common sense realized that it was part of woman's periodic cycle and therefore a temporary lapse and would cheer herself and say,

"Tomorrow is another day."

"It's one of her off days. You can always tell." It was a survival of the fittest and blessed with that spark of independence Val never weakened.

This November day Val was up early as she intended to skin the rabbit before she went to work. They were all tired of sow belly pork and Pat Rice had saved her a plump rabbit. That, and some suet dumplings would be a welcome treat for this cold blustery day. This time of the day she felt particularly lonely, it was dark and cold and she had a hatred of crossing the yard in the bitter frosty air. She gathered her skimpy nightdress around her legs before the poorly burning fire and mused on days gone by. Alf had gone, Bob might as well be gone, and now Oliver Hendley. She had so missed his handsome, intelligent features around the factory yard. She had hoped desperately that she would get to know him better, a close relationship with such a wonderful person would have been paradise. She sighed as the thought spelled out, 'Man proposes, God disposes.'

Val had met and negotiated with Harry's aunt to make arrangements for Harry to come to live with Val's family. When Auntie Hattie said the boy must decide, Val was thrilled to know that he had decided to establish himself with Val and her family, telling her that his father had expressed his wishes that his future would be secure and happy with his already adopted mother. Her sole reason now was living to comfort and support her growing family. ,

CHAPTER NINETEEN

A FRIEND IN NEED

It was during these winter months that Val's patience and stamina was sorely tried. Val and Emmie who could exist on nothing, like a desert eagle, were working before the fire in the ill lit back room. Val was not able to use the front room, for one thing, it was almost bare and even the back room did not afford much luxury, only bare necessities. They were podging away at the pegged rug and the transparently harmless widow asked,

"How is her like?"

"Topsy? Yes her legs are much better. Her steps are now straight and strong. Your tip did the trick Emmie."

"There's a piece of boiling bacon I've brought you Val. Put a cabbage with it. You'll have a good dinner. Did you know Maria's girl out of Izod's Yard had got consumption? She looked white as a split bone when I saw her last. Maria said she hadn't any clean sheets to put on the bed when Dr. Houghton called so she tore a piece off the old ones and just had enough to make a brave turn back on the bed to appear clean. I don't know if the doctor noticed it."

"If he did his profession would forbid him to remark on it. They are a wonderful band of men. They don't push for payment seeing genuine hardship. They deserve all the rewards, but I'll wager there's not many coming from Izod's Yard." Val observed.

"Our foreman at Morrell's asked me today what I'd got for my lunch. I thought he wanted some, but he said,

"Mind the work, if it's jam it will bind it together." I thought if we had the chance of a tea break, even ten minutes we could eat our 'snap' in comfort, but, as you know, Val, we has to eat it as we go on working."

"They say that Rose Parnell from Bentley has got nine months hard labour for smothering her baby. They said an appeal would be made as in this horrific case they were both starving hungry."

Val's work had drawn ahead of Emmie's so the rug was hoisted and turned to advantage in an effort to finish the outside border. Emmie asked,

"Where's Mary?"

"She's gone to Treadgold's to see 'Peg of the Pavement' or something equally lurid. She's gone with Sadie Ross. They'll be back shortly or I'll want to know why," Val warned.

"I's treated myself to a new flock bed Val. They let you pay a shilling a week at Mauntons. Have it now pay later he said, so that's what I'm doing."

"I'll see if I can get a square of oil cloth off him for the front bedroom. It's not easy trying to keep the boards clean," Val said.

"Our Bill's had raging toothache all night, but I can't afford the one and sixpence to have it out. He's threatened to put a piece of string on it and tie it to the door and slam it if it gets worse."

"Sounds painful," Val said in sympathy.

"Shall we call in Grannie Ross's tomorrow. See what's going for threepence. Our Edward needs a new jersey badly. For myself, I'll have to manage until Christmas. Sarah will lend me her dolly until I can afford a new one. It seems colder here than at the farm. It might be me gettting older, but life seems much harder here."

"According to the Indicator the council are talking of extension of housing sites at Webheath."

"Yes. I saw that, and on March fifteenth they changed the name of the main lane into Heathfield Road. It comes under the Rural District of Bromsgrove. I only hope that they provide more space than these back to back places."

"They says there will be bathrooms and water closets."

"That would be perfection. Just imagine Emmie having your own bathroom and water closet. I hate to hear that dirt cart coming around at night."

"I can hear your Mary," Emmie listened closely, but Val was already miles away blending colours for an imaginary bathroom.

"Yes, it's Mary," Val said coming back to earth, I can hear her shouting 'Good night' to Sadie."

When Mary came into the room she immediately asked why the gas wasn't alight.

"We're saving money. Isn't that right Emmie? We're planning a trip to Granny Ross's. Did you like the picture?" her mother asked.

"Yes. They sung a lovely song called, 'Goodbye', we had a good weep" Mary said.

"Had a good weep? You could have stayed here in the yard and had a good weep. That's entertainment?" Val queried.

"It will be better next week. There's a live play at Kingfisher Hall in Worcester Road. Maria Martin in the Red Barn." Mary groaned and playfully tried to strangle her mother.

"Sloppy things, you and Sadie. Put the kettle on and make some tea, Emmie's thirsty. We've been slogging away on the rug."

"I'll give you a hand later," Mary promised. "By the way mam young Mr. Sisom's coming to see you tomorrow night, Mary said casually. Val startled, rang out,

"Whatever for? Why is he coming here? You haven't done anything wrong?"

"No, no, he just told me he wanted to see you on an important matter. He said about seven o'clock."

"Well you know what this yard's like on Friday nights. But I don't see why he couldn't have made arrangements to meet at work in the office. Anyway the young ones will be in bed by then and you and me can prepare some supper. I suppose it will be alright. This rug will be finished by then and perhaps you can lend me a couple of chairs Emmie. Is that possible?" Emmie nodded and Val said,

"Thanks a lot. But you'll have to be home early our Mary and give me a hand to tidy the back room." "He's ever so nice mam. He always stops for a chat when he passes through the packing department."

"Yes. I had noticed his interest in your work. Perhaps you are set for a rise."

"Until he came so close I didn't realize what deep blue eyes he had." Mary's voice saddened. "But he is painfully shy mam, and has a dreadful stammer. Perhaps it's due to his war service. He took some letters from me on Monday and his hands were like ice, but his smile goes deep inside you." Mary remembered.

"They say in the office that he has succeeded to a title from a distant cousin who remained unmarried."

"So if he is an earl or baronet or whatever I can't see why he should want to come here" Val wondered.

"Well. That's how he told me mam. I'll help you make the house look spic and span before I go to Sadie's house. She told me her brother William wants to take me a walk through Muskett's Woods on Sunday night. Will that be alright with you mam? They've invited me to tea. Can I go? He's a fine lad, although Sadie says he's turned religious since the war started."

104

"Yes. I know Sadie's mother. She takes in the factory washing since the Lavender Laundry closed down. We'll walk up Oakley Road with Emmie. Got your coat Emmie? Thanks for the bacon. It'll do for tomorrow. I'll pay you Friday. I'll have plenty to do."

CHAPTER TWENTY

THE PROPOSAL

The next day Val had left Mary to dish out the porridge while she sewed on the missing button on Tom's overcoat and repaired once more the backside of his breeches. 'Boys' she thought. He was always so quiet indoors. Strange when he returned home you would have thought he had battled with the whole school single handed. Nevertheless, there were no early morning blues here for Val felt a shade more cheerful at Mary's unexpected news. Val sighed at the thought of so many tasks to be completed before evening. She ran to get in the vegetables from the scullery and as she passed by close to Mary she paused a second and kissed the top of her eldest daughter's head.

"That's a refreshing smell. New shampoo?"

"Yes, it's Amami. For fine hair. I'll do yours tonight when I get home."

Mary gave one more stir, then lifted the pot from the open fire saying,

"There's enough porridge here for Edward and Tom. Topsy and me will have some bread and milk. I've made you some dripping toast, mam. Don't worry we shan't be late."

Bright beams shone from the well polished grate as a result of Val's earlier enthusiasm and already a smell of steamy soap suds invaded the back room from the 'whites' scalding in the brew house. Val felt unnaturally light and frothy, almost a touch of hysteria but, holding on to Mary's arm going up Unicorn Hill later the dark brown mood had completely vanished, as Val said,

"As one door shuts another opens." Could be Mary was in for a better position. She possessed an alert brain which was necessary for the swift calculation of figures. The more refined conversation of office employment would fulfil Val's ambition for Mary. Anyway they could but wait and see the result of the proposed visit.

Life suddenly appeared too smooth to be real. She had

experienced this mood before. Too good to be true blues. 'Curiously,' Val thought 'we hunger for happiness, then when it comes, so unaccustomed are we to the brightness that we yearn for the shadows, lest the gleam should so sear our feelings that we may experience a more serious blow." It was late in the afternoon that Mr. Sisom senior verified that his son Graville would be calling on Val.

"Mr. Sisom. Why can't I see him here in the office?" asked the puzzled Val.

"Well, Val, this matter has nothing to concern our factory only in a very roundabout way. This is an important private matter, if that is convenient to you."

"Yes, yes. I'll be pleased to meet him. But, as you know, we are only working folk. We haven't the grand background of your circle."

"Val, Graville is so changed since he returned from the war. He's gone through the mill. Never discusses the details, but I can hazard a guess at the reason for his changed ideals. Truly he has his priorities right, but I'm very disturbed lest it should be a fleeting phase and that the horrors he's seen have given him a slightly unbalanced view of life. He wants to change everything at once. Makes me tired merely listening to his ambitions. His enthusiasm is overwhelming. It is genuine, but will it last? His intentions are to stand for Parliament supporting the new Labour Movement. Better houses, better education and factory conditions.

Hope he doesn't burn himself out. I appreciate your commonsense, and you will understand my meaning when you hear him talk. Perhaps you can make him ease up. We need calm, clear dedicated public spirited members to produce our Brave New World Val. I think he's arranged to call this evening so, if you can chase these orders by three o'clock, you may leave early and attend to the children's needs. If that will be of assistance to you dear."

"Thanks Mr. Sisom, you are exceptionally kind. That would help, but Mary managed to cover most tasks early this morning, but I will gladly take advantage of your offer hoping Graville will partake of a meal with us. " Val swept across the town picking up some new bread on the way from Watkins, also a packet of Symmingtons Soup, as she understood all wealthy people began a meal with a plate of soup. This seemed such a waste to Val. Waste of time, effort and money, for the soup Val made for her healthy family was a meal in itself. Nevertheless, she intended to do the right thing for her guest and even lashed out on a bottle of orange squash.

Coming down Unicorn Hill she saw smoke coming from her house, as soon as she opened the door she sensed something was taking place. A cheery fire was well alight and more coals were placed in the coal bucket. Noises came from the sitting room. Val went straight through and opened the shabby through door. Emmie, with a pair of men's thick socks covering her slippers was polishing vigorously a new square of red and gold linoleum. Placed either side of the fireplace, although set out but not yet alight, two pretty chintz covered fireside chairs were placed, and in the centre of the room Val's little table, covered in a lace tray cloth boasting a bowl of marigolds.

Before Val could utter why or how, Emmie explained "I ordered the square of lino you wanted Val and our Bill brought down these two little fireside chairs. You can borrow them until the weekend."

"How can I thank you? It's grand. I was ashamed of this room, but in no time at all you've transfigured the scene. That will be far better to entertain our boss. Hope the fire lasts out. I don't usually have two fires going at the same time. Let's have a cuppa Emmie. You deserve it, even if I haven't been here to help. I really think you've made a grand job of the room. I'll pay you back someday my wench."

"Don't mention it Val. That's what neighbours are for." After tea Val kissed little Emmie lovingly and thanked her profusely before she hurried away. Val sat alone in the tiny back room wondering the real reason for Graville Sisom's visit. Her mind was in a whirl. She would set a match to the sitting room fire as soon as he arrived. It would be a better outlook from the sitting room window, for, being a corner house there was a yard or two more garden and Val had planted it with cuttings from here and there, and, at least, there was the fresh green tracery of the lilac tree giving shade and privacy against the window. It wasn't usually pleasant at the rear of the house when Millie Summers came back from the pub swearing at the children and kicking the cat or her out of work husband, which ever got in her way first.

By now the children were safely tucked up in bed. Mary had disappeared, but promised to be back in an hour. Val's thoughts were interrupted by a knock at the back door. Already several children were gathered around the smartly dressed gentleman shouting where No. five was. Val rushed to save him from further embarrassment and showed him into the front room. The lavender scent from Emmie's wax polish did give a refreshing fragrance to the room. Val lit

the fire and he stretched his hands out to the blaze. He was
a fine soldierly looking young man and at his faltering words
Val's heart went out to him and bade him make himself at
home. He looked around the room in astonishment,

"Mrs. Thomas you have made a paradise here for your
family."

"Thank you Mr. Graville" Val resisted the temptation
to explain the boring details and he said understandingly,

"I'm sure it wasn't easy. Only someone practical and
dedicated could have done it."

"With some help of course I have my darling Mary.
Can I get you a drink? We have some very potent parsnip
wine. Real vintage. Or would you rather have orange
squash?"

"To be quite frank Mrs. Thomas, I'd prefer a cup of tea.
We suffered many ordeals in the war with the help of a cup
of tea. 'The drink that cheers but not inebriates' he quoted.
But, first, may I wait until I've explained my call."

"Now for it," thought Val. He was indubitably
nervous which puzzled Val. Truth to tell, the appearance of
the tall, proud woman so elegant against the poverty stricken
background was so unlike the personality he had anticipated
to meet. Having never had the opportunity to meet her at
the factory, was obviously disconcerted to open his speech.
At last he began,

"My dear lady. You are so kind to give me this
welcome. You will think me dreadfully selfish when you
understand the reason for my proposal. You see I love your
daughter Mary." Val was knocked sideways and paled
visibly at the implication of his statement. What did the
man expect? But before she became too overwhelmed, he
put his strong arm lightly around her thin shoulders and went
on quickly to assure her,

"Mrs. Thomas, Val. I want to marry Mary. Her charm
is dynamic and her calm passive nature has (unknown to her)
enslaved my senses. You may think otherwise, but I am
not a rich man. Yes, I have inherited a title and a grand
house, but the callousness of war has impoverished the
building. It needs a fortune to set it to rights. I expect my
father has explained I am standing for the new Labour Party.
I felt desperate and depressed when I first came home to see
the neglect and decay. Then I met Mary, then, I saw the
sweetness of a spirit I'd been searching for, and I knew
immediately in which direction my destiny lay. My father
is sceptical but realizes now, the single minded sincerity of
my promises. Of course, Mary will be offered a place at
a finishing school for a couple of years. We could be married

soon after at Ipsley Church. There is a cottage in the grounds of Woodcote Hall which would be put at your disposal, after it is renovated to your own taste. Eventually the house will be opened to the public and your talents would be put to good use in the gift shop. The boys could also contribute in that direction, seeing that Harry and Tom are throbbing with energy, they can both go to town on the carpentry section. Of course they must clear all the schooling hurdles first." He was glad when his speech ended and still looked ill at east. Val was supremely happy but thoughtfully asked,

"Have you asked Mary?"

"No. I'll ask her tonight if I have your permission. I promise you I'll give her more love than her dear heart can hold."

"Well, Graville, for myself, I see no reason whatsoever to raise any objections to your honourable and gallant proposal, but Mary is sensible enough to know where her affections and devotion will be nurtured. We'll see her response. In the meantime how about that cup of tea?"

Mary came home about eight and helped Val prepare the simple meal and afterwards, when Val ushered them both into the sitting room she informed Mary that Mr. Graville had a proposal to make. She left them well alone to make their decision.

The remains of the meal was cleared from the table and when the couple emerged some time later arm in arm and shyly smiling, all Val's agonies of insecurity, fears and disappointments rolled away like snow off a mountain.

Graville kissed Val on the cheek and whispered,

"I'm so happy. Mary has said 'Yes' now all we need is your permission."

Val looked from one to the other as two silly tears rolled down her cheeks.

"Forgive me. I never realized it possible to be so happy. Of course I give my permission. You are a truly honourable young man and I know my Mary will be secure in your good hands." Mary held out her arms to her mother saying,

"Thanks, our mam."

THE END